Picture *Perfect*

Also by D. Anne Love

Semiprecious

The Secret Prince

The Puppeteer's Apprentice

Margaret K. McElderry Books

Margaret K. McElderry Books
New York • London • Toronto • Sydney

Margaret K. McElderry Books
An imprint of Simon & Schuster Children's Publishing Division
1230 Avenue of the Americas, New York, New York 10020

Book design by Krista Vossen
The text for this book is set in Baskerville.
Manufactured in the United States of America
2 4 6 8 10 9 7 5 3 1
Library of Congress Cataloging-in-Publication Data
Love, D. Anne.
Picture perfect / D. Anne Love.—1st ed.
p. cm.
Summary: When her mother leaves her family suddenly to take a new job, fourteen-year-old Phoebe tries to deal with her own confused feelings and, in the process, learns some things about love and the complicated ties that bind families together.
ISBN-13: 978-0-689-87390-4 (hardcover)
ISBN-10: 0-689-87390-5 (hardcover)
[1. Family problems—Fiction. 2. Interpersonal relations—Fiction.
3. Family life—Texas—Fiction. 4. High schools—Fiction.
5. Schools—Fiction. 6. Texas—Fiction.] I. Title.
PZ7.L9549Pic 2007
[Fic]—dc22
2006003508

For Sarah

Heartfelt thanks once again to the entire creative team at McElderry Books, and to my agent, Maria Carvainis.

Picture *Perfect*

A week after my fourteenth birthday my mother, who sold lipsticks, moisturizers, and soaps for Bee Beautiful Cosmetics, submitted the winning entry in the company's product-naming contest for a new conditioner. Like all of the Bee Beautiful products, it featured honey as a main ingredient. Besides the honey it was chock-full of vitamins and natural herbals and was supposed to tame even the most unruly head of hair. Mama named it "Bee-have!" The president of the company called Mama to give her the good news, and after that she was on her way to the annual Bee Beautiful convention in Las Vegas, all expenses paid.

I went with my daddy and my brother, Zane, to take Mama to the airport. My sister Shyla, a chronic overachiever who had set a goal of becoming the youngest lawyer in Texas, was at the university down in Austin, churning out her prelaw course credits and working as a barista at Jazz-n-Java, a coffeehouse on Sixth Street that Shyla said was interesting as all get-out due to the clientele. On any given night she might be serving double espressos to state senators, local musicians, cross-dressing head cases, or aging hippies who had moved to Austin way back in the 1960s and never left.

"It's too bad Shyla couldn't come," Mama said as we neared the airport. "I miss my girl."

Mama looked prettier than ever in her Bee Beautiful makeup and a jonquil yellow suit with a sparkling diamond bee pin on the lapel, the prize she'd won the year before for selling more Bee Beautiful products than any other beauty consultant in Texas. And despite missing my sister, Mama seemed all keyed up and thrilled to pieces to be heading off for her prize trip.

"Shyla will be home in a couple of weeks," Daddy reminded her. We pulled into the short-term parking lot. Daddy parked the car, and he and Zane dragged Mama's four oversize suitcases to the baggage check-in.

"Jeez, Mom," Zane complained as the suitcases rumbled and bumped over the walkway, "how come you need so much stuff? You'd think you were going away forever."

Mama laughed. "Five days is a long time when you need outfits for half a dozen meetings and dinners."

We got to the baggage check-in. Mama showed her e-ticket receipt and her ID to the attendant, who tagged her bags, handed her a boarding pass, and wished her a good flight.

"Well," Mama said to us, "I guess this is it."

Daddy kissed her cheek, being careful not to smear her makeup. "Have fun, Beth. You deserve it."

"Oh, I'm going to have a fabulous time!" Mama said, pulling Zane close. "Zane, honey, you look after your sister, and don't drive that car too fast."

"I won't." Zane squirmed away before Mama could kiss him.

She pointed her finger at him, and I recognized the shade of her nail polish. Reckless Rose. It had arrived in the April shipment of Bee Beautiful products along with Tangy Tangerine and Perfectly Peach. "Remember to fasten your seat belt. Every single time, Zane. I mean it."

"O-*kay*! I'm not an idiot."

"I know. But you haven't been driving all that long. It doesn't hurt to be reminded."

She turned to me. "Phoebe darling, I'm just as sorry as I can be to miss the mother-daughter tea, but I promise to make it up to you if it's the last thing I do."

Pulling me close, she kissed the top of my head. I leaned into her, closed my eyes, and breathed in the familiar smells of Bee Beautiful perfume and breath mints. If I had known what was about to happen, I'd have held on to that moment a little longer, but I pulled away and said, "Bye, Mama. See you next Saturday."

Daddy said, "Beth, you'd better go. The security

line is getting long, and you don't want to miss your plane."

I stood there with Daddy and Zane, smiling and waving until my arm about fell off. Mama stepped onto the escalator and rode up to the departure area, leaving behind nothing but the faint scent of her perfume.

Daddy took Zane and me to lunch at a steak place near the airport, and we drove home to Eden, never dreaming that all our lives were about to be changed forever.

The following Thursday, Mama called and said the big shots at Bee Beautiful wanted her to stay a little longer to talk about a wonderful opportunity, and that she'd be home in another week. When that week stretched into two weeks, Daddy tried to pretend that she'd come rolling into Eden at any moment and everything would go back to normal. But after Mama called again to say she'd accepted a fabulous job in Las Vegas as a national Bee Beautiful spokeswoman, and to please box up her clothes and send them out, he stopped pretending.

That afternoon I found him sitting on the floor in the middle of their bedroom, Mama's shoes and skirts, and the fur jacket he'd given her last Christmas, piled around him, looking so bewildered, so full of hurt and loss, that I wanted to cry. Don't get me wrong, I loved my mother a lot, but ask anybody in Eden and they will tell you I've been a daddy's girl from the get-go. Even Mama herself said that Shyla was her girl but I belonged to Daddy. She said that when I was a baby, I'd sit in my high chair and cry for him after he left for work in the morning. Maybe I could tell even then that I'd grow up to be tall like him and somewhat of a natural on the basketball court. I lost interest in playing in seventh grade and hadn't gone out for a team since, but I still loved hanging out with Dad and watching his beloved Chicago Bulls on TV, even if they weren't quite the same after Phil Jackson left to coach the Lakers and Michael Jordan retired to star in commercials for hot dogs and underwear. Basketball was the way we connected; it was the part of Daddy that was all mine.

He patted the floor and motioned me down beside him. "Hey, Feebs."

"Hey, Daddy." Ever since my twelfth birthday I'd been trying to train him to stop calling me Feebs and use my real name, but under the circumstances I wasn't going to correct him.

He picked up Mama's jacket. "Remember last year? Remember how she pretended to faint when she opened the box on Christmas morning?"

Of course I remembered, but I didn't want to. I didn't want to remember anything.

"She'll come back," I said. "Once she gets Las Vegas out of her system."

"Yeah," Daddy said, even though he didn't believe

it either. "This spokeswoman job is good for your mother. She's been feeling sad lately."

"Lately" was really the two whole years since Shyla had graduated from Eden High and moved to Austin. My sister was nineteen now, and Mama could see her firstborn going out to meet her future, moving farther and farther away. More than once I'd wanted to tell her that me and Zane were still here trying to survive teenhood and needed her more than the überstudent Shyla ever had. But I hadn't said anything, and now Mama was gone for who knew how long.

I helped Daddy fold Mama's things, and we got some boxes from the attic and packed everything up. Then he went into his study, where he kept his law journals and casebooks, and shut the door.

*

Now it was June. School was out for the summer and Mama was still gone, still running around all over the country teaching other women how easy it was to Bee Beautiful.

There wasn't much to do in the summer in Eden, Texas. Zane and I planned to spend our vacation driving around in the ten-year-old Ford my daddy the judge had given Zane for his sixteenth birthday, swimming at the lake, and just hanging out while we waited to grow up so our real lives could begin.

Daddy spent most of his time downtown in his courtroom, where he had developed a reputation for sorting out all kinds of disagreements. People said that no matter how complicated and messy a case became, Sumner Trask could think on it and figure out what should be done to make things right. But when his wife went AWOL, leaving him to deal with two teenagers all by himself, he was at a total loss. I guess it's always easier to fix other people's problems than your own.

It was a hot Saturday and I was home alone. Daddy was playing golf with a couple of lawyers, and Zane was down at Threadgill's Garage, supposedly repairing the dents in the Ford, but I suspected it was mostly to hang out with Mr. Threadgill's daughter, Ginger. She was in Zane's class at school and had been our neighbor until last year, when her daddy moved them to a house out on the Dallas highway to be closer to the garage. Ginger was a strawberry blonde, not fat, but not thin, either. I guess you'd say she was solid. Zane said she could fix a flat tire without even breaking a sweat and was the only girl he knew who could explain rack and pinion steering, or tell the difference between a socket wrench and a screwdriver.

I made myself a glass of iced tea and took it out to the porch. The full weight of summer in Eden was settling in; cicadas whirred in the trees, the air was heavy and still. Normally I loved summer, but this year, with Mama Lord-knew-where, Shyla consumed with her prelaw summer school classes, and Lauren Braithwaite, who had been my best friend since third grade, living in Atlanta because her dad had taken a new job there, I was left to face the entire summer without anyone who understood what it was like to be a fourteen-year-old girl.

A black car pulled into the driveway of the vacant house next door, where our elderly neighbor, Mrs. Archer, had lived until she broke her hip and had to go stay with her daughter in Houston. Now there was a FOR SALE sign in the weedy yard, and I'd made a habit of checking out the potential buyers. I watched as a real estate saleslady ushered her client up the front steps and unlocked the door. I was ready for something exciting to happen. I hoped that whoever moved into Mrs. Archer's house would shake things up and change my life.

Be careful what you wish for.

Another boring Saturday arrived. Daddy got up early to take the Lincoln to Threadgill's for an oil change. Zane left for a swim meet right after Dad, banging the door on his way out, gunning the Ford's engine as he pulled onto the street. After they left, I switched on the TV and flipped through the channels while I ate a bowl of Wheat-O's, but there was nothing on except cartoons and a gloom-and-doom announcer talking about the death of more soldiers in Iraq. I don't know why the news always has to be so negative. Just once I'd like a day in which nobody gets shot, no kids go missing, and no country starts the morning off by blowing another one to kingdom come.

A delivery truck pulled into our driveway. The driver got out and unloaded a bunch of bright yellow boxes. Mama's monthly shipment of Bee Beautiful products had arrived. I went out to the porch, signed for them, and carried them into the hall. The sight of those boxes made me miss her so much I could hardly stand it.

I left the Bee Beautiful invoice on her desk in the den. The phone rang and I picked it up. "Hello?"

"Good morning!" said a woman in the relentlessly cheerful voice required of all Bee Beautiful consultants. "I'd like to speak to Beth Trask."

"Me too," I said, and hung up.

Just then a commotion started up outside, and I went out to the porch. A moving van had pulled up in front of Mrs. Archer's house, and right behind it was a baby blue convertible piled high with suitcases.

A pretty, dark-haired woman wearing an enormous pair of sunglasses, pink shorts, a white blouse, and sneakers got out of the car. She ran up to Mrs. Archer's door, unlocked it, and motioned to the men in the van. They started carrying in furniture: a white sofa, a couple of yellow-and-white-striped chairs, and a coffee table with a glass top that reflected the blazing Texas sun.

"Amazing, isn't it?" said a honeyed voice that made me jump. I'd been so intent on watching the furniture parade I hadn't noticed that the woman had crossed the yard and was standing at the bottom of our porch steps. She pushed her sunglasses to the top of her head and smiled up at me. She had a killer tan and eyes the color of violets. She looked so perfect that it was hard not to stare.

"Ma'am?"

She swept one arm toward Mrs. Archer's porch,

which was now buried under a mountain of boxes. "Amazing how much stuff a person accumulates in a lifetime. I don't need half of it, but I couldn't bear to throw it out." She held out her hand. "Beverly Grace."

"Hi." I shook hands with the woman with two first names. "Phoebe Trask."

"Phoebe! What a beautiful name." She looked past my shoulder. "Is your mother home? I'd like to meet her."

"She isn't here."

"Too bad. I was hoping she could give me some advice on where to shop. I've been out of the country for so long I'm out of touch with all things American."

"Where did you come from?"

"Italy. A little town just outside Florence." Beverly shaded her eyes and watched the moving men staggering up the porch steps with a stack of flat wooden crates. "Oh, I hope they don't drop my paintings!"

The men made it inside, and Beverly said, "They hate me."

"Who, the moving guys?"

She nodded.

"How come?"

"Book cartons," she said as the men returned to the truck for another load. "There's nothing heavier than books. I gave away a ton of them before the move, but there were certain ones I couldn't give up, you know?"

I nodded. Up in my room was a complete set of Nancy Drew and Anne of Green Gables books I hadn't cracked in years, but I liked knowing they were there in case I ever wanted to. Beverly leaned against the porch railing like she had nothing better to do. The moving men went back and forth, taking in box after box. When the house filled up, they started stacking boxes on the porch.

"You want a soda or something?" I asked.

"A soda would be lovely," she said. "Thanks."

I went inside and got two cans of cola, filled our glasses with ice, and took everything outside on one of Mama's white wicker serving trays. Beverly poured cola into her glass and took a long sip, watching me over the rim of her glass. I smoothed my hair and hoped I didn't have a milk mustache or a piece of dried cereal stuck to my face. I was dying to know why anybody would give up an exciting life in Italy to move to a nowhere town like Eden, but I didn't want to be rude.

Beverly rattled the ice in her glass and, like she could read my mind, said, "I was born in Fort Worth and lived there until I was ten. When my daddy died, my mother and I moved to Georgia to live with my grandparents. After college I worked in New York for a while and then moved to Italy." She smiled. "When it was time to come home, I just felt like Texas was where I belonged."

"How come you picked Eden?" I asked.

Just then the van driver waved a stack of yellow papers and yelled, "Hey, lady! We're all done here."

Beverly handed me her glass and stood. "Will you excuse me, Phoebe? I need to write these guys a check. But I'd love to meet your mom later."

"Sure," I said. "Later."

She ran back across the yard just as Daddy drove up and got out of the car. "Hi, hon. New neighbors?"

"Her name is Beverly Grace."

Daddy watched Beverly take her purse from her car, then lean over the hood to write a check. Her silver pen flashed in the light. She said something to the van driver, and he laughed. Maybe I should have seen trouble coming then, from the way Daddy's eyes followed her as she walked back to the house, but I didn't.

Beverly went inside, and Daddy unlocked the trunk of his car. "Help me with these groceries."

We carried everything in and later boiled hot dogs for lunch. After we ate, Daddy poured himself another glass of tea and switched on the TV. The Texas Rangers were playing an afternoon game; it was the top of the sixth inning, and they were up five runs to four. He scooted over to make room for me on the couch, but I never was much of a baseball fan because the game unfolds so slowly. I loved the quicker pace of basketball, where one fast break, one jump shot at the buzzer, can spell the difference between a loss and a win.

"Where's your brother?" he asked, fiddling with the remote.

"Swim meet at the Y."

"That's right. I forgot."

Which pretty much summed up my father's relationship with his only son. With Shyla, Daddy talked law and her plans for law school until I thought I'd die of boredom, but at least he talked to her. With me it was mostly about basketball or what was happening at school, but he and Zane hardly ever talked, except when Zane asked for permission to go somewhere or needed to borrow gas money. I felt bad for my brother, squeezed in the middle between Shyla and me. Shyla got to have our parents' undivided attention until she started preschool, and I got more than my share because I was the youngest, but Zane never had the chance to be the center of attention for very long. He was only twenty-two months old when I came along and took over as the baby of the family. He could have hated me for that, but instead we became best buddies. Mama would pack up our favorite toys and take us to the park or the swimming pool, and we'd play for hours, inventing our own games or building forts and castles with Zane's blocks. We hardly ever fought, although one day he got mad at me and beheaded my favorite doll, and I retaliated by flushing his goldfish down the toilet. Mama made us apologize to each other and sent us to our rooms for the whole afternoon.

But being separated was such torture we climbed out our bedroom windows and sat on the roof playing "I spy" until Daddy got home from the courthouse and talked us down.

Now, with Daddy engrossed in the Rangers game, I poured myself some more tea and went out to the porch. Beverly came out and started dragging boxes into the house. She waved me over. "Phoebe. How would you like to earn ten bucks?"

"Sure."

"Help me with these book cartons."

We dragged the cartons into the living room, which still held a faint smell of Mrs. Archer, a combination of mothballs and peppermint. A couple of hours later, Beverly shoved the last carton into the entry hall and dusted off her hands.

I looked around. Considering that she'd just moved in, the house was really tidy. In the living room the white sofa and yellow-striped chairs were arranged around the fireplace. Empty bookshelves sat against the wall. A bouquet of silk flowers and several silver picture frames were grouped on the coffee table. A bunch of flattened moving cartons leaned against the far wall.

"I just cannot abide clutter," Beverly drawled. "I can't write a word until everything is unpacked and put away. The sooner these boxes disappear, the sooner I can get back to work on my book."

I'd never met a writer before. I'd always pictured writers as pale, messy looking, and bleary eyed from staying up all night smoking French cigarettes and writing poetry nobody understood. But Beverly Grace looked amazing, even after a day of carrying boxes and unpacking crates.

"What's it about?" I asked.

"Mileva Einstein," Beverly said. "The genius behind the genius. Hardly anyone realizes what a huge part she played in working out the theory of relativity. People give Albert all the credit. It's time someone told her side of the story."

"Anybody home?" Daddy called from the porch.

"In here!" Beverly yelled. "The door's open!"

Daddy came in and handed Beverly a glass of iced tea. "I thought you might be thirsty."

"I am way beyond thirst," Beverly said. "My mouth is so dry I couldn't make spit if my hair was on fire."

Daddy laughed, and I realized what a long time it had been since I'd heard that sound. "I'm Sumner Trask, Phoebe's father."

"Judge Trask!" she cried. "It's such an honor to meet you. I wrote a piece for the *International Times* about a case you decided last year. *Harmon v. Harmon*? Very interesting." She held out her hand. "Beverly Grace."

It was the first time in all my fourteen years of life

that I had ever seen my daddy blush. "Thank you. That case presented a unique set of legal considerations. I enjoyed the challenge."

Beverly drained her glass. "Oh, that tastes so good. Real Southern iced tea like my Georgia grandmother used to make."

Daddy looked pleased. "The secret is in the sweetener. I use simple syrup instead of granulated sugar."

"That must be it," Beverly said. "You'll have to give me the recipe, although I am not much of a cook."

"It's just water, sugar, and fresh mint," I told her. I was getting mad at Beverly for flirting with my father. And mad at Daddy for letting her flattery get to him. "It isn't hard."

If Beverly sensed my feelings, she didn't let on. She smiled and handed Daddy her empty glass. "Thanks. I was saying to Phoebe earlier today that I hope to meet your wife soon. I think it's important to know one's neighbors, don't you?"

"Beth has been traveling quite a bit lately. We don't see nearly enough of her these days, do we, Feebs?"

When I didn't say anything, Beverly fished a ten out of her purse and handed it to me. "Thanks for helping me out, Phoebe. Maybe you could come back tomorrow and help me organize my books."

"We'd be happy to," Daddy said. He stood there holding her lipstick-smudged glass and grinning like he'd just won the Texas lottery.

I glared at him. "I thought you were watching the ball game."

"Rangers won."

He turned to Beverly. "Since your kitchen isn't unpacked yet, why don't you come over for breakfast in the morning?"

"That's very nice of you, but I couldn't," Beverly said. "It's too much of an imposition."

"Daddy," I began, "if she doesn't want to come—"

"No trouble at all!" Daddy said in his courtroom voice, which settled everything from arson cases to where to go for dinner. "I make pancakes on Sundays. Come at eight."

"All right," Beverly said. "But only if you let me bring something."

"We're out of orange juice," I said.

"Phoebe!" Daddy said.

"Well, we are. You forgot to buy any today."

Beverly laughed. "I'm going shopping anyway. I'll pick some up."

"We'd better go," Daddy said. "See you tomorrow, Beverly."

Beverly stood at the door and watched us cross the yard to our house. When we got to the porch, Daddy turned around and waved. She waved back.

And that was how it began.

Chapter Three

The next morning a muffled whine, interspersed with thumping sounds, woke me. At first I thought it was Zane messing around in his room, but then it hit me. Daddy was running the vacuum cleaner. I squinted at the clock on the dresser. It was only a few minutes after six, and the judge was into major housecleaning. Well, the house could use a sprucing up.

Not that we lived like those animal hoarders you see on the TV news where the cops go in after somebody dies and find millions of cats and years' worth of tin cans and newspapers stacked up everywhere. Daddy said we were clean enough to be safe, and dirty enough to be comfortable. But since Mama left, we'd let things slide a little. We didn't polish the furniture every week the way she had, and we waited until the sink was full of plates and cereal bowls before loading the dishwasher.

Zane's room had been declared a toxic waste area even before Mama left, and as for me, I didn't make my bed every day even when she was around, unless she forced me to. It's such a huge waste of time, since you're just going to mess it up again a few hours later.

The vacuum cleaner noise died with a long, final whine just as Zane tapped on my door. Three short taps, the code we'd invented almost as soon as we learned to talk. "Come on in!" I said. "I'm awake."

Zane, barefoot and bare chested, came in and made himself at home on my beanbag chair. He stretched out his legs and raked the hair out of his eyes, and I was struck all over again with how cute my big brother was. It could have made him arrogant, but Zane wore his good looks in an offhand way that made him seem almost shy. He had lots of female friends, people like Ginger Threadgill and Caroline Harte, whose twin brother, Will, managed the swim team, and all the dates he wanted, but he didn't really have a serious girlfriend. He yawned and said, "What's with the judge?"

I filled Zane in on everything he'd missed the day before, including Daddy's obvious infatuation with Beverly Grace and the fact that she was coming to breakfast.

"Well," Zane said, standing up. "I guess I'll go hang out at Will's place. I'm not up to making small talk with some boring writer person."

"What happened at the swim meet? Did you cream the competition?"

He grinned. "I won both my individual events. The team came in second overall."

"That's great! Did you tell Dad?"

"He wouldn't care," Zane said, shrugging. "Plus he was already in bed when I got home last night. It's no big deal. These summer meets are just to keep us in shape for next season." He ruffled my hair. "But thanks for asking." He turned to go, then said, "Hey. You want to ride out to the lake with me later? I'm meeting Ginger and a couple of guys from the team."

"Sure! That would be great."

"Okay, then. Later."

He opened my door just as Daddy came up the stairs wearing a faded Texas Longhorns T-shirt, a pair of plaid Bermuda shorts, and one of Mama's aprons, a white one with yellow cupcakes printed all over it.

"Interesting fashion statement, Dad," Zane said. "Martha Stewart meets Homer Simpson."

"Glad you approve," Daddy said. "I need your help getting some serving platters out of the garage, son. They're in that blue plastic bin next to the Christmas decorations." He glanced at his gold watch, a present from Mama a few years back. "Look at the time! Let's get a move on." He peered at me. "You, too, sunshine. Beverly will be here soon, and there's still a lot to do."

"Whoa," Zane said. "Slow down, Judge. She's just a neighbor, and you're a married man."

Zane said it like he was joking, but I could tell that

my brother was dead serious. I found myself in silent agreement. It didn't take a rocket scientist to see that my father and Beverly Grace were attracted to each other. And even though I figured the chances of Mama's coming home anytime soon were roughly a million to one, I still hoped it would happen before Daddy gave up waiting for her and moved on.

"I'm just being neighborly, Zane," Daddy said. "I hardly need a lecture from you. Go get those platters, okay? And Feebs, please set the table. I'm going to hit the shower."

Zane rolled his eyes as I said, "Okay."

"And use the good dishes. Not the ones with the roosters on them. They're chipped."

He headed for his bathroom, and Zane shook his head. "God. Why is he acting so weird?"

"I guess he misses having a grown-up around." We headed downstairs. "Maybe Dad and Beverly will hate each other after they get to know each other better."

Zane frowned. "I don't think so. Not after the way you said she fawned all over him about that big case he decided last year. It sounds to me like she's starstruck."

"Oooooh, Judge Trask," I mimicked. "It's *such* an honor to meet you!"

"Please," Zane said, heading for the garage. "I haven't had my breakfast yet."

In the kitchen I got the step stool from the pantry and took Mama's blue-and-white plates from the top shelf of the china cabinet. By the time I had set the table in the dining room, Daddy was out of the shower and dressed in a pair of pressed jeans, his favorite brown cowboy boots, and a white shirt with the sleeves rolled up. He put the coffee on and measured the pancake flour, whistling to himself. I poured maple syrup into Mama's cut-glass pitcher and left it in the microwave to be heated at the last minute.

Zane came in with two white serving plates. "I thought I'd never find them," he said. "They weren't where you said, Dad." He set them on the counter. "There you go. I'm out of here."

Daddy paused in his preparations and said, "I'd like you to eat with us and meet Beverly. It's the polite thing to do."

"I have plans," Zane said, grabbing a banana off the counter. "Big day at the swim meet yesterday, in case you're interested."

Daddy cracked an egg into his mixing bowl and took the milk from the fridge. "Of course I'm interested! How did it go?"

"I won," my brother said, heading for the stairs.

Daddy said, "Get dressed, son. And wear something nice. I don't want you looking like a street urchin in front of our new neighbor."

Zane whirled around. "I told you, Dad. I'm splitting."

Daddy set his spatula down. "You do not have my permission to leave."

"Why not? You barely even notice when I'm around, unless it's to criticize me for something."

"That's not true."

"It *is* true! You never have trouble talking to Shyla, or even Phoebe, but you don't say more than five words to me unless it's to issue some edict or remind me of how I've disappointed you."

"I'm not disappointed. I just want you to—"

"Let him go, Daddy," I said quickly. "He can meet Beverly later."

Daddy held up both hands in a gesture of surrender. "Fine, Zane. Go."

Zane ran upstairs. Five minutes later he was out the door, his car rumbling down the street. Daddy pulled the pancake griddle out of the cabinet and stated the obvious: "I don't understand that boy at all."

Once, after Zane and Daddy had had a particularly loud fight, I asked Shyla why Daddy seemed so mad at our brother all the time, and Shyla said it was because Daddy had counted on his only son following in his footsteps, first as a basketball star and then into the law. But Zane had picked swimming as his sport of choice and was more interested in crankcases than court cases. Shyla said Daddy felt rejected and that was why he hardly ever went to Zane's meets. And to be honest, Zane knew which buttons to push to send

Daddy over the edge, and sometimes he said stuff he didn't really mean just to irritate the judge. Still, I admired Zane for having the guts not to give in to Daddy's expectations and to map out his own plan for his life.

The Sunday edition of the *Eden Daily Enterprise* thumped onto the sidewalk. I went out to retrieve it and glanced over at Beverly's. A stack of flattened boxes was piled on her porch. Two side windows were curtained with pink flowered sheets. The convertible was gone.

I took the paper inside, dropped it onto the just-polished coffee table in the living room, and headed for the shower. I dug through my closet for something clean to wear and came up with a pair of navy shorts and a white T-shirt. I finger-combed my hair into place and dabbed on some lip gloss just as the doorbell rang.

Daddy opened the door and Beverly breezed in. "Good morning!"

"Hey, Feebs!" Daddy yelled as if I were completely deaf and couldn't hear the doorbell. "Beverly's here!"

I went downstairs.

"Hi, Phoebe," Beverly said. "Don't you look cute as a button!" She handed Daddy a carton of OJ, then gave me a flat blue box done up in miles of white satin ribbon. "I brought you a present."

"Why?" The word slipped out before I could stop it.

I caught Daddy's frown and hastily added, "Thank you!"

"It's from Tiffany's," Beverly said, "the one in the old movie."

Shyla and I had seen *Breakfast at Tiffany's* one winter during Movie Classics Week at the Eden Theater, so I knew Tiffany's was an expensive store. I ran my fingers over the satin bow.

"Aren't you going to open it?" Beverly asked.

I untied the ribbon and lifted the lid off the box. Inside was a tiny gold seashell suspended from a delicate chain. It was so gorgeous I went speechless.

Beverly said, "In ancient times people collected seashells as a way to prove they had traveled to faraway places. Now they're symbolic of all kinds of journeys."

Daddy peered over my shoulder. "It's beautiful, Beverly, but you didn't have to bring a present."

"But I *wanted* to." Beverly took the necklace from its cotton nest and unfastened the clasp. I turned around, bent my knees, and held my hair off my neck so she could fasten it. "I first saw this necklace a couple of years ago and loved it so much that I bought a few to keep on hand for special people."

I wondered how I could possibly mean anything to her, since we'd just met, but I managed another "Thank you," and we moved into the kitchen. While Daddy poured batter onto the pancake griddle, I stole a glance at my reflection in the glass door of the china cabinet. The gold shell at my throat winked in the light coming through the window. I'd never before owned anything that made me feel so elegant.

Daddy flipped pancakes and stacked them onto one platter, the bacon onto another. I heated the syrup in the microwave. Beverly poured the coffee and orange juice, moving around our kitchen like she belonged there. We carried everything to the dining room, which we usually used only for Christmas and Thanksgiving. Daddy held Beverly's chair, and we sat down. To a stranger passing by we would have looked like an ordinary family sitting down to Sunday-morning breakfast: father, mother, daughter. Picture perfect. Except that the wrong woman was sitting in my mother's needlepoint chair, sipping coffee from of one of her best china cups.

Beverly studied the oversize family portrait hanging on the wall behind Daddy's chair, the one we'd had taken at the beach the summer Shyla graduated from high school. We were all barefoot and dressed alike in bleached denim jeans and white shirts. Mama, Shyla, and I were decked out in matching shades of Bee Beautiful lipstick (Pretty in Pink) and nail polish (Watermelon Ice). Normally, Mama was the official family photographer, but that year she'd wanted something special. The picture had turned out so well the photographer displayed it in his studio window as an advertisement and gave Mama an extra eight-by-ten copy as a thank-you gift.

Beverly said, "What a lovely portrait, Sumner! I didn't realize you had two other children."

Daddy speared a forkful of pancake. "Shyla's my eldest. She's planning to get a law degree at the University of Texas. Zane is sixteen."

Beverly turned to me. She had a way of looking at you with a stillness that made you feel like you were the most important person on the planet. "What about you, Phoebe? Are you planning to follow your father and sister into law?"

"I haven't decided yet. I'm only going into ninth grade this fall."

"There's no hurry," Beverly said. "That's what high school is all about. Exploring different subjects, figuring out what you're good at, what you like to do."

Daddy got up to refill the coffeepot. When he came back, Beverly said, "Tell me, Sumner, what's it like being a judge?"

It hurt me to see how grateful Daddy was to have somebody interested in his life. I wondered how long it had been since Mama paid any attention to the things going on in his world. When I was much younger and Daddy was still practicing law, he and Mama would talk for hours about his cases. Sometimes she would listen to him rehearsing his closing arguments and tell him how she would vote if she were on the jury. But when I was in third grade, Daddy became *Judge* Trask, and Mama became a beauty consultant. After that she was too busy demonstrating products, taking orders, and talking on the telephone to new customers to listen to Daddy.

". . . can be frustrating," Daddy was saying when I tuned back in to the conversation. "But I'm still old-fashioned enough to believe in the majesty of the law."

He poured himself a fifth cup of coffee. Or maybe it was the sixth. "I don't believe we've ever had a writer living in Eden before," he said. "What brings you here?"

"I'm working on a couple of books, and I'm behind schedule. I wanted a quiet place to work, but someplace not too far from a good airport. My real estate agent found Mrs. Archer's charming house, and it seemed like the perfect place to settle down."

Then Daddy launched into the entire history of the town, beginning with its founding in 1882, explaining that it had once been a trade center for half of east Texas, until the railroad line was built twenty miles farther west, leaving Eden high and dry. He talked and talked, as if a dam had broken inside him, unleashing a torrent of words. It was almost time for lunch before Beverly checked her watch and stood up. "Good gravy! I can't believe I've taken up your whole morning. You should have stopped me, Sumner!"

"I enjoyed it," Daddy said. "Give me a few minutes

to clear away this mess, and Phoebe and I will be over to give you a hand with your books."

Beverly grinned sheepishly. "I'm all finished. I couldn't sleep last night, so I figured I might as well get things organized. You know how it is, the first night in a new place."

I thought back to the summer after sixth grade, when Lauren and I went away to camp for the first time. We had talked of nothing else for weeks, but the reality didn't live up to the hype. The food was terrible, the lake was coated with scum, and you had to take a flashlight and walk down a dark path to go to the bathroom. That first night the sounds of night birds and the insects constantly batting against the window screens about drove us crazy. We hardly slept at all.

Beverly said, "By Saturday night I'll be ready for a break from my work. Why don't you all come to dinner at my house? I can't promise anything as delicious as your pancakes, but people say my fried chicken isn't too bad."

"Sounds great," Daddy said. "But I'm taking Zane and Phoebe to Shreveport on Saturday."

I stared at him. Shreveport? Since when?

Daddy went on. "My wife phoned this morning, and—"

"Mama called? And I missed her?" Mama had been so busy with her new job that any time she called home was a treat that never lasted long enough.

"You were in the shower," Daddy said. "But don't worry. She'll call back later. You can talk to her then."

He turned back to Beverly. "Beth is conducting a sales seminar there this weekend. It's a chance to see her and take in the crawfish festival. There's good food and great music. When the children were little, we used to go every year. You ought to come with us, Bev."

Bev?

"It sounds like loads of fun," Beverly said. "But I wouldn't want to intrude."

"We'd enjoy your company," Daddy said. "And Beth would enjoy meeting you. She used to write quite a bit herself. Poetry mostly."

I stood there dumbfounded at this new fact about my mother. I wondered whether there was a part of herself she'd purposely kept hidden, or whether she had told me she was a poet at heart and I'd been too caught up in the details of my own life to remember it.

"All right," Beverly said. "You talked me into it. But only if we take my car."

"It's a deal." Daddy walked her to the door, and they talked some more, their voices twining together in the summer air.

"*Ciao*, Phoebe!" Beverly called a few minutes later.

We scraped the dishes and left them in the sink. Daddy went into the den to watch a ball game. I messed around in my room, impatient for Zane to come back so we could drive out to the lake. I got into my swimsuit and threw on an oversize T-shirt that Shyla had brought back from a rock concert a couple of years before. I checked my e-mail. There were two messages from Lauren, mostly about picking out paint for her new room at her house in Atlanta and a trip she'd made with her mom to a fancy shopping mall in Buckhead. I wrote her back about Beverly's moving in next door, about my new necklace, but not about how well Beverly and my father were hitting it off.

It was nearly four o'clock before Zane finally pulled into the driveway and honked the horn. I yelled bye to Daddy, told him not to wait on us for supper, and ran outside.

"Hey." Zane was definitely in a much better mood than when he left the house that morning. He turned the radio down as I slid into the front seat beside him. "How was breakfast?"

"She and Daddy talked practically the whole morning." As he backed out of the driveway, I fastened my seat belt, gave my brother the gist of the conversations, and showed him the necklace Beverly had given me.

He whistled softly. "Holy cow. Tiffany's. That's pretty expensive."

"I know. I can't understand why she'd give such an

expensive present to a perfect stranger, unless she's got an ulterior motive."

"Such as?"

"I think she really likes Daddy and wants to get on his good side."

"Huh. Maybe she should have given *him* the necklace."

We pulled out onto the highway, heading for the lake. "There's even bigger news," I said.

Zane put his blinker on and zipped past a dump truck. "What?"

"After you left this morning, Mama called, and she wants us to come to Shreveport next Saturday to see her. She's got a meeting there."

"No way!"

"Way. And get this: Daddy invited Beverly to come with us."

"Is he crazy? Mama will go ballistic."

"That's what I thought too. But Daddy told Beverly that Mama would be tickled to death to meet her because Mama used to be a poet. Did you know that?"

"Nope."

A few minutes later we reached the turnoff for the lake and bounced along the rutted road that wound through a stand of pines. Zane parked next to a mud-spattered Jeep. We got out, and Zane took a grocery sack from the trunk of the car.

"What's in there?" I asked.

"Stuff to make s'mores," Zane said.

We walked down the grassy path to a concrete pavilion next to the water. Ginger and Caroline were already there, stretched out on a pair of air mattresses. Me and Zane dumped our stuff onto the picnic table.

"Hey," the girls said.

Caroline shaded her eyes with her hand. "How's it going, Phoebe?"

"Okay."

Caroline's brother, Will, arrived with another guy from the swim team. Zane made the introductions, and the boy called Ryan set an ice chest on the table. "Anybody want a soda?"

He passed them around and said, "Hey, Zane. How about a race?"

"You're on," Zane said. "You coming, Will?"

Will said, "You girls want to come and watch?"

It seemed to me like more fun than just sitting around, but Ginger said, "No, thanks. We'll stay here and guard the food."

The boys headed down to the cove, leaving me with Ginger and Caroline. They were both really nice, but they were two years older than me, which is no big deal when you're five or nine or twenty-six, but when you're fourteen, it's the Great Wall of China. Ginger and Caroline were going to be high school juniors. Already they were stressing about their SATs and college applications, whereas my biggest worries were whether I would find my locker and whether the teachers would like me. Aside from the fact that we all adored my big brother, we had little to talk about.

I sat on the picnic bench and sipped my cola. Across the water I could see kids jumping off the pier, yelling as they hit the cold lake. I looked for Zane and his teammates, but they had gone in the opposite direction, where they wouldn't have to dodge the casual swimmers. Caroline and Ginger were talking about people I didn't know, so I swam for a while, idly paddling back and forth near the shore.

Finally Zane and the others returned from their race, dripping wet, sand sticking to their bare legs. They were laughing, breathing hard, teasing one another about who had won.

"Let's eat," Will said, grabbing a grocery sack from beneath the table. "I'm starved."

We made a fire in the pit next to the picnic table and roasted hot dogs over the flames. When those were gone, Ginger said, "Time for s'mores! I've been looking forward to them all day."

While we roasted marshmallows, Will jogged out to his Jeep and came back with his boom box. He popped a CD in and turned up the volume.

Zane pulled on a T-shirt over his swim trunks and plopped down between Ginger and me. The fire crackled and sent a shower of sparks into the air. "Having a good time, Phoebe?" he asked.

"The best." This was the most magical time on the lake, when the water reflected the dark shapes of the trees, the croaking of frogs wove through the dark, and flickering campfires circled the water like a golden necklace. The scene reminded me of other times at the lake, before our family split apart. I wished for those old times again, but I was learning it was a mistake to want anything too badly. Start feeling like you can't live without something, and the next thing you know, it'll be taken away.

We ate s'mores, washing them down with soda, until Ryan stood up. "It's been a blast, but I gotta go. Curfew."

Will jumped to his feet and doused the campfire. "Yo, Romeo and Juliet," he called to Zane and Ginger, who had wandered off and were leaning toward each other like the stems of flowers, whispering in the dark. "The light through yonder window breaks. Time to go home."

We packed up and headed for our cars. Zane and I followed Will's Jeep back up the road to the highway. Caroline and Ginger were behind us in Caroline's ancient Beetle. At the intersection Zane tooted the horn. We turned left and started home.

I reached for the radio, looking for our favorite late-night disc jockey, but Zane said, "Don't, Phoebe. Leave it off."

"What's the matter?"

"Nothing! Do I have to give you a reason for *everything*?"

"Are you still mad at Daddy?"

"No more than usual."

"Did you and Ginger have a fight?"

"Not exactly." He blew out a long breath. "Maybe. Oh hell, I don't know."

"You want to talk about it?"

Zane ran his hand through his hair. "It's a big mess. Junior prom is almost a year away, but Ginger and Caroline are already all over it. I thought Ginger was hinting around for me to ask her to go with me, so I did. Then she tells me she's not sure; she really likes Ryan, and she doesn't consider me a potential boyfriend."

"*What?* You could have fooled me, the way she was holding on to you all night. Plus you guys have known each other forever."

"That's the problem."

We were approaching the Eden city limits; Zane slowed down and went on. "Ginger thinks I'll never see her as anything but a friend, and maybe she's right. I'd feel awful if I talked her out of dating Ryan and then found out we really don't click as a couple."

"Maybe you're just worried that if she falls for Ryan, you'll lose her as a friend. Or maybe it's true love. Do your palms sweat? Do you feel sick to your stomach, dizzy sometimes, like you just came off a ride at Disneyland?"

Finally he laughed. "Shut up, wiseacre."

He pulled into our driveway and killed the engine. The light in Daddy's study blazed brightly, but the rest of the house was dark.

Zane said, "Is Dad still mad at me for not hanging around this morning?"

"I don't know. After Beverly left, he watched the Rangers game and made a bunch of phone calls. He seems pretty excited about seeing Mama."

We got out of the car. Then the porch lights came on and the front door opened. Daddy pointed to his watch as we came up the steps.

"Cutting it close tonight, I see. It's two minutes to eleven."

We went inside, and Zane made a beeline for the stairs. "I smell like the lake. I'm hitting the shower."

Daddy locked the front door and turned off the porch light. "Did you have a good time, Feebs?"

"It's *Phoebe,* Daddy. And yes, it was great."

He pulled me close and kissed the top of my head. "I was starting to worry about you."

"We have a cell phone. We'd have called if there was trouble."

"I know," he said. "I'm just lonely, I guess. This house seems too big these days."

"She'll come back," I said. "She has to."

He nodded and turned back toward his study. "Good night."

I went up to my room and stripped out of my damp clothes. I desperately needed to talk to Shyla about Beverly, about what was happening with Daddy, about my upcoming meeting with Mama. I burrowed into my bathrobe, and while I waited for my turn in the shower, I placed an emergency call to my sister.

The next Saturday morning Beverly rang our doorbell at eight sharp. Daddy had been up for at least an hour; I'd heard him bring the paper inside while I was still in bed, and now the smell of fresh coffee was wafting up the stairs. I was up and dressed. Zane was awake; I could hear his shower running. He and Daddy had had a big argument the night before. Zane didn't want to waste half his weekend driving to Louisiana and back to see Mama when it was plain to him that we were hardly a blip on her radar screen, but when Daddy gave him a choice of handing over the keys to his Ford or going with us, Zane gave in. Now he was giving Daddy the silent treatment, and my stomach was knotted like a ball of twine. Mama's birthday was just around the corner, and I'd bought her a present, a book of poems by Emily Dickinson. I wasn't sure Mama would like Emily's short, fierce poems, but as Shyla once said about the little black dress, a classic is always a safe choice.

I put Mama's present in the bottom of my tote bag and went down to the kitchen.

"There you are!" Beverly trilled. "I'll bet you're just thrilled to pieces to see your mom."

I grabbed a bagel and smeared some strawberry cream cheese on it. My feelings were too jumbled to explain, so I said, "I guess so."

Daddy shook his head and refilled Beverly's coffee cup. "You know how teenagers are."

Then Zane came downstairs, dressed in a pair of cargo pants, a white T-shirt, and sneakers, his hair still damp from the shower.

"Zane," Daddy said. "This is our new neighbor, Beverly Grace. Beverly, this is my son, Zane."

Beverly held out her hand. "Hello, Zane. I hear you're quite a swimmer."

"Hello." Zane made a point of avoiding eye contact with Daddy as he shook hands with Beverly. He opened the fridge and stuck his head in. "Any OJ?"

"On the top shelf," Daddy said.

Zane's head reappeared, along with the Florida Tropic carton. "I was talking to Phoebe."

"Zane," Beverly said smoothly, "I read in the paper about your double win at the Y last week. That's pretty impressive."

My brother chugged some OJ and fixed himself a bagel. "Thanks."

Daddy wiped down the counter, turned the coffeemaker off, and said brightly, "Okay, gang, let's get going."

I picked up my tote, Zane grabbed his music player, and we followed Daddy and Beverly out to the curb. Zane's eyes lit up when he realized we were taking Beverly's convertible, but since he was still operating in silent mode, he just slumped in the backseat next to me and plugged into his music.

Beverly tossed Daddy her keys. "You drive."

Daddy slid behind the wheel, adjusted his sunglasses, and pulled away from the curb. Beverly covered her hair with a silk scarf, tying it under her chin like Queen Elizabeth on vacation in Scotland.

We got to the freeway, and the car picked up speed. The rush of wind through the open car tangled my hair. Beverly turned around and raised her voice above the engine noise. "Phoebe? You want a scarf? I have an extra."

I shook my head. I liked the feel of the wind in my hair. Even better, I liked that the noise saved me from having to make conversation. I thought back to last weekend's midnight phone call to Shyla.

"What's the matter?" Shyla had mumbled when her roommate, Alison-from-Florida, put her on the line. I imagined Shyla sitting up in bed, pushing her hair out of her eyes, squinting at the clock.

I told her about breakfast with Beverly, about the

Tiffany necklace, and that I was worried because Daddy was paying so much attention to our new neighbor. "It feels like too much, too fast," I told her. "She hadn't known us for twenty-four hours, and there she was, looking into Daddy's eyes, hanging on to his every word, giving me presents, and telling me how special I am. I think she's after him."

"I doubt that." I could hear Shyla yawning.

"Huh. You didn't see how they were looking at each other. Don't you *care* if our parents break up?"

Shyla sighed. "They're not going to break up."

"How can you be so sure?"

"Because Daddy still loves Mama. But even if he didn't, divorces take time, even in Texas."

Her covers rustled, and I imagined her throwing off her blanket and sheets and getting out of bed to pace, like she always did when she was thinking hard about something. "Get a grip, Phoebe. The world won't end because Daddy smiled at an attractive woman."

"I think Beverly Grace picked Daddy out on purpose," I went on. "She wrote a magazine article about him last year. I think she bought Mrs. Archer's house so she could trap him."

Shyla let out a whoop so loud it about busted my eardrum. "Give the judge some credit, okay? He earns his living figuring out people's motives. He's too smart to fall for a scheme like that. Besides, how do you know Beverly isn't married too?"

"I've never seen anybody else over there."

"Well, she's only lived there for a couple of days. Maybe her husband is in the military. Maybe he's a traveling salesman. There could be a thousand reasons why he hasn't shown up yet."

"She's not wearing a wedding ring," I said. "She's probably been divorced a million times already."

"Listen, Phoebe," Shyla said in a voice that meant she was running low on patience, "I have to go. I have a ton of research to do at the library, plus a paper to finish, and I'm bushed. My relief person never showed up for work tonight, and I had to pull a double shift. I'm too tired to worry about Dad right now."

"Fine. When Mama and Daddy wind up in divorce court, don't say I didn't warn you."

"It'll be okay," Shyla said. "You'll see."

"When are you coming home?" I asked.

"I'm not sure. Maybe at the end of August, depending on whether I get an internship. But I'll call you soon."

"Shyla?"

"What?"

"I love you." Somehow it was always easier to say over the phone.

"Love you too, kiddo."

The line clicked.

Now a gas station was looming, and Daddy slowed

down. Beverly turned around and said, "Bathroom break?"

"Okay."

Zane had fallen asleep, one hand curled under his cheek, his music still playing. I got out and followed Beverly into the Gas and Go, past the candy aisle and the soft-drink dispensers and into the rest room at the back of the store. While I was in the one and only stall, I heard the short hiss of a spray bottle and came out into a cloud of White Shoulders perfume.

"I love this scent, don't you?" Beverly put on some more lipstick, swiveled the tube closed, and dropped it into her bag. She leaned over the sink, and a silver ring suspended on a matching chain spilled from the open neck of her shirt. Her eyes met mine in the crackled mirror. "It was my husband's. He died in a car crash in Rome two years ago, during a research trip."

Just as I thought. No husband in the picture. I wanted to whip out my cell phone right then and gloat to Shyla, but of course I didn't. "That's awful," I said. "I'm really sorry."

"Thank you."

She went into the stall. I left and waited for her outside. Daddy was standing beside the car, stuffing his credit card back into his wallet. Beverly came out, dug her sunglasses out of her bag, and took up the conversation right where she'd left off. "You'd have enjoyed talking to my Marshall. He was an anthropologist."

Then I was glad I'd paid attention last year in Mr. Dunham's social sciences class when we studied the work of Margaret Mead and Louis Leakey. Even though I didn't trust Beverly, I didn't want her to think I was a small-town hick who didn't know anything. "Your husband went around digging up stuff from the past," I said.

"Yes. He specialized in ancient battle sites. He found a number of human skeletons that showed evidence of mortal wounds, but his most important find was a sword that may have belonged to Perkin Warbeck."

Never heard of the guy, but I nodded like I was impressed.

"Marshall was in the process of authenticating the sword when he died."

Daddy tooted the horn. "Let's go, you two."

"Just a minute!" Beverly opened her wallet and handed me a ten. "Get us something cold to drink, will you, hon? Driving with the top down makes me thirsty."

I went back inside and bought three colas and an extra-large root beer for Zane. When I got to the car, I handed Daddy and Beverly their cups, then got into the backseat and touched Zane's cold cup to his bare arm to wake him up.

He jumped, then grabbed the drink and took a long pull on his straw. He looked at his watch.

"Another hour and a half of this. God."

"Hey," Beverly said, switching on the car radio. "How about some Louisiana festival music to get us in the mood?"

"Must we?" Zane muttered.

"Zane," Daddy warned. He put the blinker on and pulled back onto the interstate. Then we lapsed into silence until at long last we started seeing bigger towns, and signs pointing the way to the crawfish festival.

Since we weren't meeting Mama until five o'clock, we headed to the festival grounds. Daddy parked in a dusty field, and we hiked back to the entrance. As soon as we got our tickets, me and Zane split and left Daddy and Beverly on their own. While a bluegrass band twanged away on a makeshift stage, we wandered around checking out the tattoo artists, jewelry makers, and T-shirt booths, but the food was the main attraction. Zane found a table under a tree near the stage. I saved our places while he scouted for food. Pretty soon he came back with two plates heaped with corn on the cob, coleslaw, and spicy steamed crawfish, which are creatures sort of like lobsters but so tiny you have to eat a boatload of them to feel full.

The bluegrass band finished its set, and a zydeco band began playing. Several couples got up and started dancing, their boots kicking up little clouds of dust. Zane wiped melted butter off his chin, surveyed the scene, and rolled his eyes. "What," he said, "are we doing here?"

"Killing time until we can see Mama." I ate a couple of the crawfish, but my stomach was so jumpy I pushed my plate away.

Zane snorted. "Like she gives a flip about us."

"She's the one who called Daddy and invited us here. That's got to be a good sign. When she sees us, she'll realize how much she misses us."

"I wouldn't count on it." He polished off the last of his corn, wiped his hands, and crushed his paper napkin into a hard little ball.

As the song ended, Daddy and Beverly came toward us through the crowd. When they got to our table, Beverly surveyed the wreckage and said, "You obviously enjoyed your meal."

Zane stood and gathered up our trash. "I've never been too keen on mudbugs, to tell you the truth. The corn was good, though. Excuse me."

He started toward the trash bins behind the stage. I grabbed our empty paper cups and followed him. Daddy called, "Get a move on, you two. It's time to go."

All the way to the car Beverly chattered about how great the cotton candy tasted, how pretty the silver jewelry was, and how much she enjoyed the zydeco band. We got in, and Daddy started the engine. We drove back toward the hotel in town where Mama was holding her Bee Beautiful meetings and got there right on time. I went to the bathroom in the lobby to fix my hair and calm my nerves. Mama had been gone more than three months, and though she called home every chance she got, she never talked for very long. She was always rushing to a meeting or getting ready to shoot a television commercial or racing for an airport somewhere.

I wanted my mother back. As close as Zane and I were, there are some things a fourteen-year-old girl just cannot share with a boy. I needed a woman to talk to. Lauren was gone, and e-mails just weren't the same. And Shyla was usually too busy to listen. Tears started behind my eyes, but I willed them away. Something stronger than tears was needed to win my mother back, but for the life of me, I couldn't figure out what would make her give up her glamorous life and come home to Eden.

I smoothed on some Bee Beautiful lip gloss and ran a comb through my hair, which could have used some of Mama's new Bee-have! conditioner, but there was nothing I could do about it. I took a couple of deep breaths and opened the door.

Zane, Daddy, and Beverly were standing at the far end of the lobby. Beverly untied her scarf and shook out her hair. Daddy smiled at me and said, "You look beautiful, sunshine."

Then the elevator dinged, the doors opened, and

out came Mama with two other women. They were dressed alike in pastel suits with diamond bees on the lapels. The other women smiled at me as they headed for the reception area, but all I could see was Mama. She was thinner, and there were dark circles under her eyes, but she was dressed as beautifully as ever, in a moss green suit and a pair of high heels that looked like they cost as much as a Volkswagen. Her cell phone and day planner peeked from the top of her briefcase. She was carrying a huge white shopping bag with gold writing on it.

She crossed the lobby at a fast clip, her heels clicking on the marble floor. When she got to us, she dropped everything, kissed Daddy, and opened her arms wide to Zane and me. "My darlings!"

Like we were the ones who had left, instead of the other way around.

"How are you?" Mama asked. "My heavens, Zane, I swear you have grown a foot taller." She hugged us hard, then stepped back, holding us at arm's length. "Oh, if only Shyla were here, this would be just perfect. I have missed you all like crazy."

But not enough to come back, I thought.

Then we were all talking at once, but Mama's eyes kept darting from us to the two Bee Beautiful ladies waiting at the reception desk, and I realized that even as she was asking about Zane's swim meets and how my summer was going and if I'd heard from Lauren since the move, she couldn't wait to get this reunion over with and go back to her new life.

Finally, when the initial excitement had died down, Daddy broke into the conversation and introduced Beverly. He told Mama that Beverly was a writer and that she had bought Mrs. Archer's house.

"Daddy invited Beverly to come with us," I said.

"Did he?" Mama glanced at Daddy and then smiled her professional Bee Beautiful smile. "Mrs. Grace, it's a delight to meet you. Tell me, what does your husband do?"

"I'm a widow," Beverly said. "For two years now."

"I'm sorry." Mama acted cool as a cucumber, but I could see that the idea of Daddy's living next door to a beautiful widow had shaken her up some, so I decided to make her worry a little more.

"Beverly had breakfast at our house last week, and she gave me this necklace." I fished it from beneath my T-shirt. "It's from Tiffany's. It's real gold."

For a moment my mother lost the power of speech. She looked at Beverly, then back to me, and finally said, "Well, Phoebe, that's very nice. Although it's much too insubstantial for a girl of your height. Tall girls should wear heavier pieces. Pieces with presence."

It was like getting slapped. My eyes swam with tears.

Daddy said, "For Pete's sake, Beth. She's just a teenager."

Zane squeezed my shoulder. "I think it looks great on her," he said.

"Well," Mama allowed, "I suppose you can get away with it while you're young."

Then she grabbed the shopping bag off the floor and said, "I brought you something from California."

She handed Zane and me a couple of boxes, and we opened them. I got a pair of L.A. Girl jeans, a pink tank top, and a couple of CDs. Zane got a sweater and a very expensive book that had been on his Christmas list for two years running.

Mama watched us open the boxes, a smile playing on her perfectly painted Bee Beautiful lips. It was obvious she'd taken time to pick out things she knew we'd like, but an entire ton of loot couldn't fill the empty space her leaving had made in our lives. She didn't see that all the presents in the world couldn't make up for what we'd lost.

"Thanks, Mama." I put on my happy face, but I couldn't help wondering why I wasn't good enough for her to stick around.

"Yeah," Zane said. "I've wanted this book forever."

"It was nothing." Mama flapped her hand like she was swatting away a fly and said to Daddy, "Did I tell you I made number one in sales in the region? Nearly a million dollars' worth of Bee Beautiful products sold in this quarter alone!"

"Congratulations," Daddy said. "It's everything you wanted."

"Not quite," Mama said. "I've got my sights set now on being number one nationwide. And it never could have happened if I'd stayed in Eden." She smiled at me then. "There's not enough of a customer base."

One of the women at the desk called, "Beth, honey? We need to get going, or else we'll miss the shuttle to the airport."

Mama glanced at her watch. "Goodness, look at the time!"

She kissed Daddy's cheek. "Sumner. Thanks for bringing the children. You take care of yourself, you hear?"

"You too, Beth." Daddy caught her wrists in his big hands. "We miss you."

They stood there looking into each other's eyes, and my breath caught. I let myself hope she might come home with us, but then the two Bee Beautiful ladies hurried past us, dragging a ton of baggage and three huge sample cases. "Hurry, Beth!" one of them said. "We've got your luggage. We'll meet you in the van."

My heart started pounding. Mama's words had hurt me, but not nearly as much as her leaving would. I opened my tote and handed her the poetry book. "I brought a present for you, too. Happy birthday, Mama. In case I don't see you in September."

She ran her fingers over the lacy pink paper I'd bought at the card store in the mall. "Oh, Phoebe, this is terribly sweet, but I don't know where I'd put it. My bags are so full now I'll have to pay extra at the airport." She handed it back to me. "You hang on to it for me, okay?"

She kissed Zane, then pulled me close. But I didn't hug back. I let my arms dangle at my sides, as if I were a giant Raggedy Ann.

"You be good," Mama said. "And when you talk to Shyla, tell her I love her."

Tell her yourself, I thought. I glanced at Zane, and I could see that he was thinking the exact same thing.

Beverly said, "It was lovely meeting you, Beth. I can't tell you how much I admire you."

Mama beamed. "You do?"

"Oh, yes. I can only imagine how difficult it must be to spend so much time away from home. You're to be congratulated for having so neatly divided your time between your career and your family." Beverly made a chopping motion with her hands like she was cutting up a cabbage. "I'm sure I couldn't do it."

For a minute Mama looked confused, trying to figure out whether Beverly was being serious. Then she smiled and said, "Why, thank you, Beverly."

The hotel van pulled up at the entrance, and the

driver honked the horn. Mama scooped her briefcase off the floor and ran for the door. "Bye, now!"

We stood there watching until the glass doors had slid shut behind her and the van had pulled away.

"Well," Daddy said, "it sure was nice seeing her, huh?"

"It sucked," Zane muttered.

"Big time," I said.

Daddy put his arm around me. "Come on, Feebs. It's a long drive back to Eden, and we're all hungry. Once you've eaten something, you'll feel better."

My stomach was so knotted that the thought of more food made me gag, but I couldn't blame Daddy for suggesting dinner as the antidote to my hurt feelings. He couldn't help it. He'd been raised in South Carolina by his aunt Reba, one of a long line of Southern women who believed that any situation in life, no matter how dire, could be greatly improved upon by the consumption of a good meal and a strong cup of coffee.

Beverly hooked her arm through mine. "I don't know about you, but a couple of scoops of Rocky Road in a waffle cone always makes me feel better."

We left the hotel and put our presents into the trunk of Beverly's car. Twenty minutes later we pulled into Peg-Leg Brown's, a seafood restaurant with a statue of a one-legged pirate out front. We ordered shrimp, Caesar salads, and baked potatoes with the works. Daddy and Beverly tried to keep the conversation going, but Zane and I didn't feel much like talking, and they finally left us alone and concentrated on their food.

When we'd finished, Beverly opened her bag and took out her credit card just as Daddy reached for his wallet. She put a hand on his arm. "Sumner. This is my treat, now, and no arguments, please. You've been very kind to me, and I want to reciprocate."

"It's not necessary," Daddy said.

"But I want to."

Beverly signaled the waitress and handed over her card. After she signed the bill, Daddy and Zane went to get the car, and Beverly and I went to the ladies' room. As we left the restaurant, Beverly said, "Phoebe? I'm sorry about what happened today. I hope you know it was me your mother was trying to hurt with her comments about your necklace."

"Why would she want to hurt you? She doesn't even know you."

"I'm a widow living next door to her husband and children. That's all she needs to know in order to feel threatened." Our footsteps crunched on the gravel parking lot. Beverly said, "Anyone can see that your mother loves you deeply. But she loves her work, too. She wants to be in two places at once, and it makes her angry that she's forced to choose."

We waited as an SUV backed slowly out of a parking

space. "I shouldn't have made that remark about dividing her time," Beverly continued. "It was a cheap shot, and I'm sorry now that I said it, but I could see that you were hurt. I felt the whole thing was my fault and I owed it to you to even the score."

Even though I was halfway mad at Mama right then, even though her criticism and her rejection of my present had cut me to the quick, I couldn't side with Beverly against her. Still, I could see that Beverly was trying to make me feel better. "Thanks," I muttered just as Daddy and Zane came zooming around the corner and stopped in front of us.

We got into the car. Zane scooted over to make room for me, then plugged into his music. Beverly tuned the radio to a slow-jazz station, stuffed her scarf into her bag, and let the summer wind tangle her hair. She and Daddy talked and talked as the convertible ate up the miles and the sun went down over the bayou in a blaze of pink, purple, and gold.

I listened to the rise and fall of their voices mixing with the lonely strains of the saxophone and watched the flat green land gradually go dark. My mind filled with bittersweet memories of the way our lives had been when we were a whole family, back before the Great Divide. The remembering hurt so much I tried to concentrate on other things, such as the fact that freshman year was just around the corner, a new beginning with new adventures that would shape my life forever. But my thoughts always came back to my mother and the way her absence was turning all of us into totally different people.

Daddy cracked a lawyer joke and Beverly laughed. I imagined her husband in some far-off place, uncovering the evidence of old battles and old wounds, and I thought: *Maybe digging up the past, trying to save some piece of it, is a bad idea. Maybe it's better just to let it go.*

After the trip to Shreveport my mother started calling home more often. Maybe she was missing us after our short reunion, or maybe she was worried Beverly was taking her place in our lives. It was hard to tell because Mama mostly talked a mile a minute about everything that was happening with her Bee Beautiful career. The next big thing on her agenda was an infomercial on one of those home shopping channels.

"That's great, Mama," I said when it was my turn to talk. "Speaking of shopping, I'm going to need new stuff for school soon. When are you coming home?"

"I'm not sure, honey. It depends on how the TV spots go. Have you talked to Shyla? Maybe she'll come home and take you shopping. That would be more fun anyway, wouldn't it? Just the two of you?"

It most certainly would not. When it came to picking out clothes, Shyla was way too conservative and way too opinionated. Mama had her opinions too—remember her comment about my Tiffany necklace—and we usually fought about at least one item on my shopping list, but since seventh grade she had let me make most of my own fashion choices, even when they turned out to be unqualified disasters. Now that I was getting ready for high school, I didn't want to start off with the wrong look. It irked me that when I really needed Mama's fashion sense, she was too busy to help.

"I'll see if Shyla can squeeze me into her schedule," I said, and handed the phone to Zane, who told Mama not to worry, that if she couldn't make it home, he was sure Beverly would take me shopping.

But Beverly had virtually disappeared following our trip to Louisiana. I figured she was working hard writing her book. Once or twice I heard her car coming in late, and one night I caught a glimpse of her standing at the stove in her kitchen wearing a red caftan, stirring a pot with one hand and sipping wine with the other. She looked so lonely I felt sorry for her, and sorry I'd suspected her of going after Daddy.

One morning just before the Fourth of July weekend, Zane and I spent a couple of hours working on his car. After lunch he discovered he needed a part that Threadgill's didn't have, so we drove to a big auto-parts place out on the Dallas highway. We were on our way home, and about an hour outside Eden, when the driver of the pickup truck in front of us hit the brakes and swerved.

"What the . . ." Zane hit his brakes too and pulled over. A flash of gold caught my eye.

"It's a puppy!" I yelled.

"Where?" We skidded to a stop. Dust billowed up all around us.

"There! I hope that truck didn't hit it."

I ran to the side of the road and knelt beside the quivering ball of golden fur.

"Careful," Zane said, coming up behind me. "If it's hurt, it might bite."

But the puppy stirred and licked my hand. I picked it up and it settled against my neck like it knew that's where it belonged. I had wanted to get a dog forever, but Mama wouldn't let me. There was no way I was letting this one go. "I'm keeping it."

"Hold on, kiddo," Zane said. "It may belong to someone. Is there a tag or anything?"

But the little golden retriever wasn't wearing anything except an eager expression.

Zane took the puppy from my arms and turned it over. "It's a boy. And he doesn't seem to be hurt or anything."

"That truck almost smushed him. He was lucky."

"Look at the paws on this guy," Zane said. "He's going to be huge when he grows up."

"Give him back." I took the puppy, and it laid its wet nose in my palm. "I'm going to name him Lucky."

"That's not the most original name I've ever heard."

"Well, what would you call him?"

A car whizzed by us, stirring up a shower of loose stones.

"We'll figure it out later. Let's get out of here before *we* get smushed." Zane opened the car door and I got in with Lucky.

I nuzzled the puppy's warm face. He still had the milky smell of a newborn, although he weighed too much to be brand-new. Plus his eyes were open and everything.

Zane started the car and pulled back onto the road. "Don't get too attached to him, Phoebe. Dad may not let you keep him. And when Mama comes home . . ." He let that sentence trail away.

When we got to Eden, Zane pulled into the grocery store parking lot. "He needs food and stuff, but it's too hot to leave him in the car. You wait here and I'll get it."

I was so in love with my puppy and so eager to get him home that it hadn't occurred to me he'd need puppy chow, a bowl, a leash. I watched Zane head toward the entrance, thinking about how much I loved my brother. He always thought of everything.

Zane had left the engine running so Lucky and I could have the AC on. I turned on some soft music and held him up to the window so he could start getting used to his world. He pressed his nose to the window and licked it, smearing it with doggy slobber.

When Zane came out twenty minutes later carrying two plastic bags, Lucky let out a little yip and wagged his fuzzy tail. Zane tossed the bags onto the backseat and grinned at Lucky. "Don't try to snow me, buddy. I can already tell you're Phoebe's boy."

We circled the parking lot and pulled up to the stoplight at the corner. We were waiting for the light to change when a familiar blue convertible whizzed by, my daddy at the wheel. Beverly was sitting next to him, her long dark hair blowing around her face, and they were laughing like they'd just heard the world's funniest joke.

"Did you see that?" I asked as the light turned green and Zane shot onto the street.

"I saw." Zane glanced into his rearview mirror.

"What is he doing with *her*?" All my anger and suspicions came roaring back.

"He's lost his mind." Zane floored the gas pedal and we tore down the street. Stores, houses, telephone poles, passed in a terrifying blur.

"Slow down!" I yelled.

But Zane just kept driving like a maniac, weaving in and out of traffic, taking the turns so fast the tires squealed and the Ford's frame shuddered.

"Zane! You're scaring me!"

He sped past a delivery truck, past the courthouse,

made a hard right onto our street, and skidded to a stop in the driveway. He killed the engine, gave me a blood-chilling grin, and said, "We're home."

I had never seen him act so out of control. I wasn't sure which was scarier—his recklessness behind the wheel or the rage coming off him like waves of heat. "What's the matter with you?" I yelled. "Are you crazy?"

I unfastened my seat belt and cradled my puppy.

"Get off my case." He grabbed the plastic bags off the backseat and slammed the car door shut.

We went up the steps and into the kitchen. Zane dumped the bags onto the counter. "There's his stuff. Knock yourself out."

"Why are you mad at me? It's not my fault."

I set Lucky down and rummaged in the bags for his new bowl. I filled it with water, and Lucky lapped it up.

Zane turned around, his keys still in his hand.

"Where are you going?"

"I'm not hanging around here, that's for sure." He headed for the door.

"What'll I tell Daddy?"

"Tell him whatever you want. He won't care anyway."

Zane ran out to his car and sped away. I put on Lucky's collar, snapped on his leash, and took him outside. At first he pulled and balked at every step, but finally he got interested in his new surroundings. He sniffed around and peed on Mama's pink hydrangea bush, which for some reason made me feel good.

I took Lucky back inside, gave him some puppy chow, and made myself a sandwich for supper. Then I got his new squeaky ball and rolled it across the floor.

"Go get it, Lucky," I said. "Get it, boy."

Lucky just stared at me.

"Hey, you're a retriever," I told him. "You're supposed to go get stuff and bring it back."

He squatted and peed all over the carpet.

"No, Lucky! You're supposed to go outside. Not in the house!"

I got some paper towels and blotted up the mess. It smelled awful, so I put a couple of drops of vanilla flavoring on the wet spot and opened the windows, even though it was still ninety degrees outside and the AC was going full blast. "Money out the window" was what Mama always said when Zane or I left a door open in summer. But Mama was gone, along with everybody else. I figured if I was going to live there by myself, I'd do as I pleased.

Finally Beverly's car swung into her driveway next door. I heard Daddy tell her good night, and he came inside, carrying his jacket and briefcase, whistling to himself. When he saw me and my new dog, he stopped midnote and tossed his stuff onto a chair.

"Phoebe! What in the world is this?"

"He nearly got killed on the highway. His name is Lucky. I'm keeping him." I picked Lucky up and held him to my chest.

"I don't know if that's such a good idea. You'll be going back to school soon, and there won't be anyone here during the day to look after him. And you know how your mother feels about dogs."

"Since when do you care one iota about Mama's feelings?"

"Keep a civil tongue in your head," Daddy said, "or else go to your room."

"You can't make me."

I had never spoken to him that way before. Talking back to my father made me light-headed.

For a moment we stared at each other, realizing for the first time that what I'd said was true. But like a clever prosecutor examining a witness, Daddy abruptly changed direction.

"Where's Zane?"

"I have no idea."

Daddy unbuttoned his shirt collar and loosened his tie. "Suppose you tell me what's gotten you so upset."

"Where were you tonight?" Lucky was scrambling to get down, so I turned him loose. "It's after eight o'clock."

"Not that I'm obligated to account for my whereabouts," Daddy said, "but I called here around six thirty, and you didn't pick up. I figured you and Zane weren't back yet, so I finished up some paperwork, ran an errand, and grabbed a bite to eat."

"Oh. Did you eat by yourself, or did you have company?"

"Don't go there, Phoebe."

Until that moment Sumner Trask, with his absolute faith in truth and justice, had been my do-no-wrong hero. Even though I didn't have the brains or the motivation to follow him into law like Shyla, I admired him more than anything. Now my faith in him was seriously shaken.

"I'm going to change clothes," Daddy said, picking up his coat and briefcase, "and then we'll discuss the dog situation."

"Daddy!" I didn't realize I was crying until my voice cracked.

He turned around.

"Please let me keep him. I know a puppy is a lot of work, but I'm a responsible person. It's almost two months till school starts, and by then I'll have him house-trained and everything."

Lucky seemed to know that his future was in jeopardy. He waddled over and sat down on Dad's shoe, his fuzzy tail scrubbing on the floor. The judge bent down to pat his head, and Lucky looked up and smiled his goofy puppy smile. I knew then he was mine.

Zane stayed away all night. We looked everywhere for him. We drove out to the lake. We checked the pizza parlor, the movie theater, and the campground at the state park. We talked to the guys on his swim team and everyone at Threadgill's Garage. Daddy called around to all of Zane's friends' houses, but nobody had seen him.

Daddy kept questioning me, but I didn't tell him why Zane had taken off. I was still mad at Daddy too and wanted to see him suffer for the heartache he had caused me.

"That's it," Daddy said. It was nearly five o'clock in the morning, and neither of us had slept a wink. "This has gone on long enough. I'm calling the police."

But then the phone rang, and Daddy snatched it up. As he listened, the color drained from his face.

"What is it?" I whispered.

He shook his head to silence me and scribbled on his yellow legal pad. "Tell Zane I'll be right there," he said, and hung up.

"What happened? Where is he?" I asked. "Is he okay?"

"He's in jail."

"*Jail?* Why?"

"I don't have time to explain it now. I need to bring him home. Then we'll sort it out." He was moving around the kitchen, picking up his briefcase, cell phone, and keys. "This may take a while. Go to bed, Feebs. The important thing to know is that your brother is all right."

"I'm coming with you."

"No," he said in a tone that meant I had no chance to change his mind. "You're not." He headed out the door. "I'll be back as soon as I can."

I went to my room. Lucky was asleep, curled into a warm little ball at the foot of my bed. I didn't bother undressing. I climbed under the covers, so tired my eyes felt gritty, but I couldn't sleep knowing that my brother was in jail. It had to be some horrible mistake. Zane could be moody and impulsive sometimes, but he wasn't stupid. I picked up my puppy and resettled him on my pillow. He licked my hand and fell back into his doggy dreams.

I must have slept a little. I remember hearing the chime of the downstairs clock and, later, the sound of the newspaper slapping against the sidewalk and the garbage truck rumbling down the street.

At last the garage door creaked open. I heard

voices in the hallway and Zane's footsteps pounding up the stairs.

I switched on my lamp and looked at the clock. It was nearly eight. Another hour until Daddy was due in court. I was dying to see Zane and find out what had happened, but it was better to wait until after the judge had left. I flopped back into bed and slept until Lucky licked my face and woke me up.

I got his leash and took him out back. He sniffed around, rolled in the grass, then finally got down to business.

As we came back to the front porch, I saw Daddy moving Zane's car into the garage. He got out, locked the doors, and pocketed the keys. When he saw me, he said, "Zane is not to leave this house. We'll talk tonight."

Before I could ask him even one question, he headed for the courthouse. I took Lucky inside and fed him, then went upstairs and knocked on Zane's door.

"Go away, Phoebe."

But I went in anyway. Zane sat hunched on the edge of his bed, his hair lank and messed up, his eyes swollen and red rimmed from crying. He wouldn't even look at me. "I told you to go away," he said dully. "Don't you understand English?"

"Oh, I understand English, all right, and I want an explanation! Do you even care that I went totally nuts wondering if you were okay? Where were you? We looked everywhere!" I peered at him. "You look awful."

"Why, thank you."

"What happened? Daddy said you were in jail."

"He wouldn't even care, except that it tarnishes his precious reputation in this town."

"He cares. He's just mad." I sat down at his desk. "It was a mistake, right? Some mix-up at the police station or something."

Finally he looked at me. "It was a mistake, all right, but I'm the one who made it." He sighed. "I was out with Heyward Dupree and a couple of his buddies. They had just come from a baseball game and were messing around with the bats. They were drinking. I wasn't. Then Heyward got the brilliant idea to knock over some mailboxes, and they talked me into driving the car."

"You knocked down somebody's mailbox?"

I was having trouble visualizing my brother, the handsome all-American swimming star, as a juvenile delinquent.

"Not just one mailbox," Zane said. "Six of them. Out on Morse Road."

"But you were just the driver, right? And you weren't drunk. Heyward and them should be in a lot more trouble than you."

"Yeah. But then we went downtown and spray-painted some of the store windows on Hamilton Street. That's when the cops showed up." He pounded his pillow. "I was just so mad at Dad, you know? Riding around with Beverly like Mama never even existed."

"I know. He lied when I asked him where he'd been. He said he was running an errand. How lame can you get?"

"He was so mad when he showed up at the jail," Zane said. "He wouldn't even look at me. He just talked to the officers and signed some papers and brought me home. Then he said I can't have my car until further notice."

Zane raked his hand through his hair, and I could see flecks of red and green paint in it. "Two whole months of summer vacation left, and I am grounded for life."

Me too. Without Zane's wheels I couldn't go anywhere. But he already looked so miserable I didn't bring it up.

Zane said, "I was just getting ready to ask Ginger out on a real date, and now I can't."

"So she isn't dating Ryan after all?"

"They went out a couple of times, but it didn't work out. Caroline said Ginger told *her* that she really wants to go out with me."

"And now everything is wrecked."

"Totally. What I don't get is why Dad is so determined to ruin my life. It's not like I ever did anything to him."

"What happens now? Do you have to go to court or something?"

"Yeah. Next Thursday."

"What will they do to you?"

"I don't care."

"Yes you do."

"They'll probably go harder on me than the others, just because I'm the judge's kid. Otherwise people will say I got off easy because he's my dad." Zane stood up. "I need a shower, and some sleep."

I hugged him. He smelled like sweat, paint, and beer. "I am so mad at you I could kill you, but I'm glad you're okay."

"Sorry I scared you. I wasn't thinking straight."

I left him alone after that. I fixed myself a bowl of cereal and took Lucky outside. I was teaching him to come and to sit. He was catching on pretty fast for such a little guy.

Zane slept practically all day. Daddy came home with a bucket of chicken for dinner, which we consumed in total silence. Afterward he and Zane went into the den and closed the door.

The next day was the worst. Zane and Daddy were barely speaking, and I was maintaining a low profile, keeping Lucky out of the way. I was in my room reading when Mama called. Daddy picked up in his office, Zane was on the extension in the kitchen, I picked up the cordless beside my bed.

"Sumner?" Mama said after we'd all said hello. "What's the matter? You all sound so strange."

"We've had a little crisis here, Beth," Daddy said.

"What kind of a crisis? Is somebody sick?"

Zane made a sound in his throat. "It's me, Mama. I messed up."

Then, with Daddy breaking in every other second to fill in more details, Zane told Mama what had happened and that he had to go to court.

"Oh, Zane," Mama said. "I do *not* have time for this. Whatever possessed you to do something so stupid?"

"Ask Daddy," I said.

"Sumner?"

"It was just a teenage prank that got out of hand," Daddy said. "I'll be with him in court on Thursday. There's no need for you to come home."

"Yes there is, Mama," I said. "Your son needs you. We all do."

"I know that, Phoebe, and I'd like to be there, but I made a commitment to the company."

"What about your commitment to us?"

Mama sighed. "Sumner, will you please talk some sense into your daughter?"

"She's fourteen," Daddy said, as if that precluded any rational discussion.

Zane said, "Never mind, Mama. I can handle it."

"They won't send you to jail, will they?" Mama asked.

Daddy said, "Not likely."

"Well," Mama said. "This is certainly a fine kettle of fish. Not what I needed to hear just before the regional sales conference."

"Heaven forbid anything should disrupt your work!" I said.

"Listen," Mama said, "I need to go. Sumner, you call and let me know what happens, okay? And Zane? I love you in spite of this. You too, Phoebe."

Like it was *my* fault!

"We love you too, Beth," Daddy said.

And we all hung up.

When Thursday came, I wanted to go to court with Zane so he'd have somebody on his side, but Daddy said spectators weren't allowed in juvenile court. It was a lousy day anyway, dark and pouring rain. Lucky freaked when I opened the umbrella over his head, and I nearly fell down trying to hold on to his leash and keep from getting soaking wet. Later, after Daddy and Zane left, I made eggs and toast and watched TV for a while, trying to keep my mind off of what was happening at the courthouse.

Just before noon Daddy and Zane came home. Lucky ran circles in the kitchen, yipping and jumping up to get their attention. Daddy tossed his keys on the counter. Zane ducked his head, muttered something about changing clothes, and ran upstairs.

"What happened, Daddy?" I picked up Lucky so he wouldn't get into trouble.

Daddy closed his eyes and pinched the bridge of his nose. "The juvenile court judge was fair. Zane will pay his portion of the cost of replacing the mailboxes, and he and the other boys will be responsible for removing the graffiti from the store windows downtown. And he's to perform forty hours of community service."

A wave of relief washed over me, and I realized that I had been holding my breath. "But he won't have a record or anything, right? He can still be on the swim team and drive his car."

"Whether he stays on the team is a matter for his coaches. The car stays in the garage until he complies with all the court mandates. Then we'll see."

"But that's not fair! How will he get downtown and back without his car?"

"He can walk." Daddy opened the fridge. "I'm starving. Let's make lunch."

Just like that the subject was closed. I didn't see how Daddy could put all the different problems of his life into separate little boxes and pretend they weren't there. When even one thing goes wrong in my life, I can't rest until I figure out how to fix it. I helped Daddy make grilled cheese sandwiches and iced tea. I yelled for Zane to come and eat, but he hollered back that he wasn't hungry. Which was pretty unbelievable. Zane was always hungry.

When Daddy went back to the courthouse for the

afternoon, Zane came down and raided the fridge, then went out to the porch to eat. Rain dripped from the eaves and plopped into Mama's azalea bushes. While Zane devoured two sandwiches and a bag of chips, I picked at a chocolate brownie and told him about the e-mail I'd just received from Lauren. "She's going to Six Flags Over Georgia and then to a concert," I said. "I'm stuck here and can't do anything."

I didn't mean to blame Zane, but summer was slipping away and I didn't have anything to show for it.

"Don't be mad at me. Everybody else in the world hates my guts. I need at least one person who doesn't think I'm a total screwup."

"Nobody thinks that."

He snorted. "Yes they do. Dad reamed me out all the way down to the courthouse and back, and then when we were on the way back home, Mama called to see how it all turned out and took the opportunity to tell me once again how disappointed she is. Mr. Threadgill won't even let me talk to Ginger over the phone." He folded his napkin, then tore it into long, narrow shreds. "But you know what I dread the worst? All the gossip in town and the talk at school."

"School is two months away. This will be old news by then. And you know how people in Eden are. They'll talk for a couple of days, until they find some new piece of juicy gossip to chew on."

"I hope you're right."

"Besides, the Fourth of July is coming up this weekend. Everybody will be thinking about the barbecue and the parade, and having a good time."

"Maybe. This morning I heard a couple of deputies talking. There's a rumor that a bunch of war protesters are planning a demonstration at the courthouse on Independence Day. The sheriff is afraid it'll get ugly."

"Protesters are nothing new. Remember those people who showed up at the courthouse last year when the county wanted to put that new road through the middle of town?"

"Democracy in action," Zane said. "*That* is what makes America so great."

"You sound just like Daddy."

"I was being sarcastic."

I picked up our tray. "Come on. Help me load the dishwasher."

We went inside, and I forgot all about our conversation until the Fourth of July arrived and, as Daddy later said, all hell broke loose.

It started off like a typical July Fourth in Texas, with the rising of the white-hot sun in a cloudless sky and the smell of burning charcoal in the air as people fired up their grills. The annual parade was a big deal, but not as big a deal as eating barbecue, which is practically a religion in Eden. Despite what I'd said to Zane about kicking back and enjoying the festivities, I was dreading the holiday because Zane and Daddy would be spending so much time together, and how tense would *that* be? Though, surprisingly, Zane's brush with the law had brought them closer in some ways. Maybe Daddy recognized Zane's behavior as a cry for help, as the TV psychologists say, or maybe Daddy was trying harder to make up for Mama being gone.

Anyway, during breakfast Zane and Daddy talked about the fall schedule for the swim team, and my brother actually cracked a smile that wasn't meant to be sarcastic. I fed Lucky bits of my pancake, breaking them off and handing them to him under the table, until he choked and Daddy made me stop.

Afterward I walked Lucky and settled him in his playpen with a chew toy and one of my old shirts, and we drove downtown to watch the parade. Daddy parked in his reserved space behind the courthouse, and we headed for our usual viewing spot on Main Street. Everybody in town was there. Kids from school stood in a tight knot on the corner, laughing and teasing one another. A couple of girls from last year's English class waved to me. I waved back but stuck close to Zane as we made our way through the crowd of parents with toddlers in strollers, old people with umbrellas unfurled to ward off the sun, and a bunch of parents in band booster shirts carrying cameras. As we took our place on the sidewalk, several people came by to talk to Daddy. Some of them just wanted a chance to stare at Zane, who crossed his arms over his chest and stared back until they moved on.

One of the sheriff's deputies stopped to talk to Daddy, and while they were comparing notes, Zane elbowed me and muttered, "Look who just showed up."

Beverly was standing across the street talking to a guy in a business suit and dark glasses. With everybody else dressed in shorts and flip-flops, he stuck out like a sore thumb.

"Must be from the Mafia," I said.

"Maybe he's her boyfriend," Zane said. "Maybe now she'll let Dad alone."

I inched my way a little closer to the curb, hoping to block Daddy's view of her.

A whistle blew and the Eden High School marching band led off the parade.

"There's Ginger," Zane murmured to me as the woodwinds section marched by, followed by a Volkswagen full of clowns and a red convertible carrying Meribeth Culpepper, the current Eden Sweet Potato Queen.

Behind Meribeth came the Lions Club float and then a float from the Eden Garden Club, complete with a giant watering can and several ladies holding straw baskets filled with real flowers.

"The one in the green dress is Caroline's mom," Zane said as the float went past. Behind the garden club ladies came a group of elementary school boys in their blue-and-gold Cub Scout uniforms, marching along with their den mother.

A popping noise erupted behind us. At first I thought it was firecrackers until somebody yelled, "He's got a gun!" and a bare-chested man in a crew cut and tattered jeans raced across the street, nearly knocking down the members of Miss Patricia's School of Dance, who were marching along in their red-and-white spangled costumes. A woman screamed, and people started shoving their way through the crowd. The parade broke up as the band members ran for cover. Miss Patricia herded her dancers onto the sidewalk, and the den mother hurried her Cub Scouts into the drugstore. A couple of sheriff's deputies tackled the man and took away his gun.

It seemed like the group of flag-waving protesters who suddenly overran the courthouse steps had come out of nowhere. Later the paper would say there were only thirty people or so, but when it was happening, it seemed like a lot more. They were chanting, "No more war!" and punching the air with their fists.

A bunch of men from the old soldiers' home started yelling at the protesters, then somebody threw a punch, and all at once the whole town started shoving and cursing, choosing up sides. The police and the county sheriff's deputies waded into the melee with bullhorns and ordered people to go home.

"Let's go!" Daddy tried to elbow his way through the crowd to get me and Zane out of there, but people were bunched so tightly we couldn't move. A couple of protesters set a flag on fire and cheered while it burned.

Then the agitators smashed the courthouse windows, and the air filled with the smell of gasoline. Flames licked the windows, and a cloud of black smoke billowed up. People began to run. Someone shoved me so hard I nearly fell. A man in Bermuda shorts and a red ponytail spilled soda down my back and stomped on my foot. Despite the chaos Daddy held my hand in a bone-crushing grip. Caught in the crowd, I couldn't see a thing.

"What's happening?" I yelled above wails of approaching fire engines and police cruisers.

"The courthouse is on fire," he said calmly. "Come on, let's get out of here."

"This way, Dad!" Zane yelled, and we cut through an alley behind the barbershop and down a side street littered with deflated balloons and crushed soft-drink cups, some of them still oozing soda and ice.

Before we could make our way back to the courthouse parking lot, the fire engines arrived, and right behind them, a news crew from the TV station. The police and sheriff's deputies were busy arresting people and herding them into white vans parked at the curb.

One of the deputies looked up as we made our way past. He jerked his thumb at a group of scowling protesters sitting in the vans. "Looks like you've got your work cut out for you, Judge."

Daddy nodded, and we cut across the lawn to the parking lot. I was impatient to change out of my sticky shirt and cool off, but we got caught in a huge traffic jam and spent an hour inching along the street, stopping every few feet to let groups of pedestrians cross or a police car pass. By the time we got home, the phone was ringing. Reporters from newspapers and TV stations all over Texas were calling Judge Trask looking for quotes about what should happen to people who burned the flag and tried to destroy a government building.

Daddy told them all the same thing: that no matter how repulsive we thought their actions were, the Constitution guaranteed free speech for everyone, and everyone was entitled to the same protections under the law.

I grabbed a quick shower, changed clothes, and got a cold can of soda from the fridge. Lucky was going nuts, jumping up and pawing me for attention, so I took him outside. Then Zane came out, handed me his cell phone, and said, "It's Mom."

"Phoebe, honey!" she cried. "I just heard about the riot on the radio. Are you all right?"

"Some jerk spilled cola all over me and almost broke my foot, but other than that I'm okay."

Just then a stray cat streaked across the yard, and Lucky let out a high-pitched yip, his first attempt at actually barking.

"What was that?" Mama asked. "It sounded like a dog. You don't have a dog in my house, do you?"

Technically, no.

"I'm outside, Mama."

"Oh. Listen, sugar, I have to go. I just wanted to be sure you were okay. I don't know what this world is coming to. Who would have thought there'd be a riot in Eden?"

But I was thinking about more-urgent matters. "When are you coming home?"

"Soon. I'm right in the middle of taping a show for

the Beauty Network. You would not believe how sales have taken off this summer. It's amazing! Is Zane still there? Let me talk to him again."

I handed the phone back to my brother and took Lucky inside. Daddy was still giving his telephone speech, so Lucky and I went upstairs. Later Daddy went out to a barbecue joint on the highway and got ribs and coleslaw for supper, since the big barbecue in town had been canceled. He brewed up another pitcher of his famous iced tea, and we ate on the porch.

Zane stretched his legs out and sighed. "Man, what a day. Nothing this exciting has ever happened in Eden. I couldn't believe those guys would be dumb enough to set fire to the courthouse with the whole town watching."

"That's the point of a demonstration," Daddy said. "To do something so audacious it attracts attention."

"Well, they got their wish," I said. "Mama heard about it on the radio clear out in Nevada."

"And there'll be plenty more publicity when their case goes to trial," Daddy said. "Those guys know how to use the system to get their message out."

Zane poured himself some more of Daddy's excellent tea. "Will you be hearing their case, Dad?"

"Too soon to tell," Daddy said.

"I hope some other judge gets it," he said. "You

know how people in Eden are. 'America, love it or leave it.' If they think those guys are going to get away with burning the flag and setting a fire, things could get nasty."

"People have to respect the rule of law even if they don't agree with it," Daddy said. "I'm not expecting any trouble."

He got up to take our plates inside. "Who wants ice cream?"

"I do," I said. "Need some help, Daddy?"

"No, I've got it. Be right back." He went inside.

Zane checked his watch. "There's a sci-fi movie coming on TV in a few minutes. Want to watch?"

Personally, I do not care for science fiction, but with all the big events in town canceled and Zane's car still impounded, there was nothing else to do. I shrugged. "Might as well."

Then Beverly drove up in her convertible, jumped out, and ran lightly across the lawn to our house.

"Hey, Trasks!" She came up the porch steps, jingling her keys. "Quite an exciting day today, huh?"

"Yeah." Zane rattled the ice in his glass.

"Too bad the fireworks got canceled," Beverly said. "I was looking forward to it. Especially with my editor in town. I promised him a genuine small-town celebration, and then those demonstrators had to go and ruin it all."

The screen door squeaked open, and Daddy came

out with our ice cream bowls on a tray. "Beverly! Want some ice cream?"

"Hey there, Sumner."

Whenever Beverly talked to my dad, she sprinkled a little more magnolia into her voice, so his name came out sounding like "Sum-nuh." It was sickening. Beverly said, "I'm leaving tomorrow for a couple of weeks, and I was wondering if you'd mind keeping an eye on the house. I've hired a boy to mow the grass, but I need somebody to water my orchids and take in the mail."

"I'm afraid I'd kill your plants," Daddy said. "I don't have much of a green thumb. Maybe Phoebe can help you out."

Before I could open my mouth to protest, Beverly said, "Would you, hon? That would be great." She was already taking a key off her key ring. "Here's a spare key. You have to jiggle the lock a bit to make it work. I'll leave some instructions for you on the kitchen table."

I took the key, and Beverly said, "Gotta run. I haven't finished packing yet, and my plane leaves at seven in the morning."

"Where are you going?" Daddy asked.

"To England. Oxford University is endowing a chair in my husband's name." She stepped off the porch. "Thanks for helping me out, Phoebe. I owe you."

"Have a safe trip." Daddy waved to her, and we dug into our bowls of Rocky Road.

Late the next afternoon I took the key and went over to Beverly's house. I found her note on the table and watered the orchids according to her instructions. I brought in the mail—a couple of bills, a fat envelope from her publisher in New York, and a bunch of advertising junk—and stacked it on the kitchen counter. I should have left then, but I was curious. I wandered through the living room and into a room at the back of the house that she had set up as an office. Her desk was covered with files arranged in orderly stacks next to her computer. A fax machine hummed in the silence. A pair of red sandals were parked under the desk as if she'd slipped them off while working and forgotten them. An oil painting, a landscape done mostly in yellows and greens, hung on one wall. An unfinished canvas stood on an easel opposite the window. On another wall was a huge corkboard covered with memos, invitations, newspaper clippings, and photographs. A glass-topped table under the window held a framed picture of a man I assumed was her husband, and another picture of a blond-haired, blue-eyed little boy with a sprinkling of freckles on his nose. He looked like a kid you'd see in a TV commercial for bread or peanut butter.

Wondering what Beverly was writing about, I opened a folder. "Einstein's letters to his wife make mention of their joint work, and it is generally believed that Mileva contributed significantly to the completion of the theory of relativity that included gravitation as a determiner of the curvature of the space-time continuum." Boring as dirt. I closed the file and flipped through her desk calendar. Going back in time, I saw she had circled the date she'd first moved into Mrs. Archer's house and the day she'd gone with us to Shreveport to see Mama. There were scribbled notes about picking up dry cleaning, reminders about mailing stuff to her editor and returning books to the library. But the one that stopped me cold was a red circle with the letters *ST* inside. I remembered the date because it was the day I'd found Lucky on the highway. The day Zane and I had seen her and Daddy together.

ST. Sumner Trask. All the proof I needed that their meeting had not been an accident.

I flipped the pages back, leaving the calendar just the way I'd found it, and let myself out of her house. I needed to talk to somebody, but Lauren was too busy making a new life down in Georgia. I was afraid to tell Zane, afraid he might do something even worse than spray-painting graffiti and knocking over mailboxes. Shyla wouldn't care; she'd just laugh and tell me I had too much imagination. My family was coming apart at the seams, and there was nothing I could do except try harder to keep Beverly and my daddy away from each other once she got back to Eden.

A couple of days later I got a letter in the mail

from my school welcoming me to the freshman class. Stapled to the letter was a class list and a copy of the Eden High School dress code. I poured myself a glass of soda and scanned the code, which was mostly a list of stuff we couldn't wear, including T-shirts with messages on them, cropped tops, pajama bottoms, flip-flops, and anything else the teachers decided was a distraction in the learning environment.

In his letter the assistant principal urged the incoming freshmen to dress for the serious business of learning and to have fun. Apparently he didn't see the contradiction in that statement. I read through the requirements for phys ed, which Lauren always contended was just a sanctioned form of humiliation and torture, and discovered I needed a certain kind of white shorts and a pair of running shoes. I was going to have to go shopping. For the millionth time that summer I was overcome with missing Lauren. All during eighth grade we'd looked forward to starting high school together. We'd planned everything out in excruciating detail, like a couple of NASA scientists preparing for a space launch, and now I felt like the countdown had been halted, the mission scrubbed.

I left the letter out where Daddy could see it, hoping he'd demand that Mama come home and attend to her motherly duties. Instead, the night before Beverly was due back from her trip, he came into the den where Zane and I were watching TV and said,

"Hey, sunshine. How about if I drop you at the mall on Saturday morning and pick you up after my golf game? We'll grab a late lunch somewhere, just the two of us. Sound good?"

"I can't shop by myself!" I said.

"Well, of course you can," Daddy said. "How hard can it be?"

"I need somebody to give me an opinion on stuff," I said. "Freshman year is important! I don't want to show up with all the wrong clothes and be labeled a dork for life."

His eyes still on the TV screen, Zane said, "They shop in packs, Dad. It's a girl thing."

Daddy took off his reading glasses and rubbed his eyes. "Maybe Beverly will take you, Feebs. She knows style."

Which was true. Beverly dressed to kill, even if she was only going to the grocery store for a loaf of bread. But I wasn't about to give her a reason to hang around "Sum-nuh," inquiring as to whether he approved of our purchases.

"I'll call Shyla," I said. "Maybe *somebody* in this family can find time for me."

Daddy nodded and put his glasses back on. Another Trask family problem solved.

The next day Daddy dropped Zane and me at our favorite burger place for lunch. People in Eden say it's just a hole in the wall, but the guy who runs it, a gray-haired Vietnam vet named Gus Parker, makes the best burgers on the planet. He doesn't fancy them up with blue cheese or pesto sauce, the way some restaurants do. A Gus burger is meat, mustard, pickles, and onions. That's it. If you insist, he will slap a square of American cheese on the meat while it's sizzling on the grill, but he lets you know it pains him to wreck his signature dish.

We grabbed one of Gus's red vinyl booths near the back and ordered large colas, burgers, and a double order of fries. The tables were jammed with construction workers, high school kids, and people who worked in the office buildings downtown.

"Here you go." Gus slid our plates onto the table along with our check. "Enjoy."

Zane bit into his burger, closed his eyes, chewed, and swallowed. "This burger is definitely worth the loss of life. Thank you, cow!"

Just then the door opened and in came Ginger Threadgill with her daddy. In her pink shorts and a white top, her strawberry-blond hair a mass of curls, Ginger looked like she'd just stepped out of the pages of *Teen Vogue*. "Don't look now," I said to Zane, "but your heartthrob just walked in."

"Oh, man!" Zane hurriedly wiped his hands on his napkin. "Mr. T. is with her, though. Talk about bad luck."

But Mr. Threadgill was so busy talking to Gus he

didn't even notice when Ginger made her way to our table.

"Hey, Zane," she said. "Hi, Phoebe."

"Hey." Zane scooted over. "Sit down."

"I can't. Daddy would have a cow, since . . . well, you know. Your problem with the law and all."

"Good gravy!" I said. "It's not like he robbed a bank. Besides, he has almost finished his community service."

"Yeah," Zane said. "I've paid my debt to society, as they say."

"I heard you were working at the library." Ginger turned to Zane. "I just wanted to tell you that even though Daddy is being totally unreasonable about it, I personally do not hold anything against you. Anybody can make a mistake."

"Thanks," Zane said. "That means a lot, coming from you."

"You're welcome."

"Ginger?" Zane paused, and I kicked him under the table. *Go on, ask her.*

"Oops," Ginger said. "Our order is ready. Gotta go."

She wound her way through the crowded restaurant and helped her daddy carry several to-go bags outside. Zane dragged a greasy fry through the pool of ketchup on his plate. "I guess that pretty much answers the question about my future with Ginger.

It's obvious Mr. T. is never going to let me live this down."

"He's just so pigheaded." I dug an ice cube out of my empty glass and crunched it with my teeth. "But he can't keep you from seeing Ginger at school."

"Yeah. You know who I blame for all of this? Our dear mother, that's who."

I felt the same way. Mama's life was working out just fine, but Daddy, Zane, and I were still struggling. "Shyla says this Bee Beautiful thing is just something Mama has to get out of her system. She won't stay away forever."

"Maybe not, but the damage is already done. Even if she came back today, nothing would be the same." He glanced at the check, left some money on the table, and stood up. "Let's go. Dad's probably waiting."

We walked outside. Daddy was sitting in the parking lot, listening to the radio. He had drawn the protesters' case after all, and the backseat of the Lincoln was strewn with files and law books.

We got in the car. Zane said, "Dad, can you drop me at the library? I want to get some more of my community service hours in."

The juvenile court judge had given Zane his choice of working on a highway beautification crew or shelving books in the library. My brother wasn't stupid; anybody who had ever spent a summer in Texas would pick a job where there was air-conditioning.

Daddy nodded, and we pulled out of the parking lot.

After we left Zane at the library, Daddy dropped me off at home before returning to the courthouse. I took Lucky outside, and later we curled up with a book in front of the TV. Ever since I'd heard that Mama was making an infomercial, I'd kept an eye on the Beauty Channel, hoping that one day she'd appear in our living room. So far it hadn't happened, but in the meantime the Beauty Channel was proving to be a real education. According to the people on TV, most of the entire female population was a royal mess, in desperate need of special fillers to hide wrinkles, lip liners that wouldn't rub off while you were asleep, sets of cutout stencils to help you draw perfect eyebrows every time, half a dozen products to brighten your smile, et cetera. It was enough to give a person a major inferiority complex.

Today a man with a ponytail was describing in a thick Spanish accent the virtues of his new line of hair care products, which were guaranteed to make even the most hopeless head of hair look thick and glossy. The phone rang. I muted the TV and picked up. There was a series of clicks, but nobody said anything.

"Hello?" I said again. "Who is this?"

I could hear somebody breathing. The heavy silence creeped me out.

"Pervert," I said, and hung up.

Chapter Eight

I was at my computer e-mailing Lauren when Beverly returned from her chair-naming trip to England. Her two-week trip had stretched into six weeks, which obviously had its upside, but I was tired of being responsible for her orchids. One had died, and a couple more were on the critical list. From my window I watched her carry a couple of suitcases into her house. Ten minutes later she came across the lawn with a shopping bag looped over her arm. I shut my computer down and called for Lucky, and we went to the door just as she rang the bell.

"*Cara mia!*" she cried when I opened the door. "I'm back!"

"Okay."

Beverly just stood there smiling until I had no choice but to invite her in. We went into the living room, and she plopped down on the sofa, fanning herself. "I swear, I'd forgotten how hot it is down here in the summertime."

Lucky yipped until she picked him up. He licked

her hand and regarded her with his big, soulful eyes.

"Hey, handsome," Beverly said, stroking his head. "You're growing like a weed." She looked at me. "How much do you reckon he weighs now?"

"I don't know. Daddy says he'll weigh around seventy pounds when he's full grown."

"How is your daddy?" Lucky squirmed and she let him go.

"Really busy," I said. "He's getting ready for the protesters' trial, and we aren't supposed to disturb him for anything."

Beverly laughed. "I know how that is."

She opened the shopping bag. "I brought you all some presents from across the pond."

"You didn't have to do that."

"Oh, I know," she said, lifting out a bunch of boxes, "but traveling is no fun unless you can bring back stuff for your friends." She handed me a box. "This is for you."

It was a pink sweater with a scoop neckline, silky soft beneath my fingers. "It's beautiful."

"I hoped you'd like it." Beverly set three more boxes on the coffee table, obviously enjoying playing Santa in August. "The red box is for Zane, and the others are for your father."

Then she took out an oblong package and let Lucky sniff it. "I didn't forget you, sweetie."

Lucky, the traitor, wagged his tail and nudged the

package with his nose. Beverly laughed and unwrapped a huge rubber bone. He grabbed it and ran to the kitchen, his toenails clicking on the wood floor.

I knew I should offer Beverly a soda or some iced tea; it was so hot I was dying for something cool to drink myself, but I didn't want to encourage her.

The front door opened and Daddy came in carrying his briefcase and a stack of mail. His eyes lit up when he saw that we had company. "Beverly! How was your trip?"

"Just lovely, Sum-nuh. After the ceremony at the university I flew to Firenze and spent some time with friends. I stayed longer than I intended, but the change did me a world of good."

"I'm glad you enjoyed yourself," Daddy said.

Beverly swept her hand toward the coffee table, like a TV model showing off a big prize. "I brought you all some tiny little presents, which you can open later. Right now I'm off to the grocery store. I don't have a thing in the house to eat."

"Eat with us," Daddy said.

"I really can't," Beverly said, heading for the door. "I must shop, unpack, do some laundry, and go through the mail." She turned to me. "Thanks for looking after things while I was gone."

"I'm sorry your orchid died. I followed your instructions, but—"

"It's all right," Beverly said. "Orchids are temperamental. Sometimes they just don't thrive no matter what you do."

I returned her spare key. She dropped it into her pocket, called out, "*A presto!*" and went home.

"*A presto?*" I said to Daddy. "She sounds like a magician."

"I think it means 'See you soon.'"

No doubt. "Why doesn't she just speak English?"

Daddy loosened his tie and sank into his favorite chair. "Give her a break, Feebs. She's spent the last several weeks speaking Italian. It'll take her a few days to switch back. Actually, I think it's charming." He flipped through the mail. "Where's Zane?"

"At the library, finishing his community service requirement. The swim team is throwing a party for him at the lake this weekend to celebrate."

"We'll have to see about that."

"That's not fair! He's been looking forward to the party all week."

"He never mentioned it to me."

"You're never around. We may as well be orphans, for all the attention we get from you."

He looked up from his mail sorting. "Have I been gone that much?"

"We hardly see you anymore. You're nearly always late."

He sighed. "Preparing for this trial is taking it out

of me, Feebs. I can't go anywhere without people stopping me to tell me just what they think should happen to the flag burners. Their lawyers and the prosecutors are running to the courthouse every day filing motion after motion, and the TV people are in my face every time I turn around. Just today that guy from channel ten jumped in front of my car as I was leaving for lunch, demanding a quote for the six o'clock news."

The phone rang.

"Don't answer it," Daddy said.

"But what if it's Mama?"

Daddy waved his hand and I picked up the receiver, but it was another one of those creepy calls where nobody said anything.

"That's the second time this week," I said.

"From now on," Daddy said, "let the machine pick up first. Even if you're expecting a call. Okay?"

Lucky trotted into the room with his new bone and stood on Daddy's foot until Daddy tossed the bone a couple of times before going upstairs to change clothes.

When Zane came home, we fired up the grill. While I made a salad, Zane told Daddy about the party that was planned for him at the lake. "Ryan's bringing a tent, and we're going to camp out overnight."

"That's not a good idea, Zane." Daddy peppered the steaks and laid them on the grill.

Zane's face twisted. "You don't trust me. I made one mistake and spent the whole summer paying for it, and now I can't do anything."

"It isn't that I don't trust you." Daddy perched on the edge of our picnic table. "Some people are bent out of shape about this trial coming up, even though it's pretty much an open-and-shut case as far as the flag burning goes. I wasn't going to tell you this, but I've received a couple of nasty notes down at the courthouse. And the hang-up calls here at home are worrisome. We should be careful until the trial is over."

When the steaks were done, he put them on the yellow platter we always used for cooking out, and we sat down. "You may go to the party, but I want you home by eleven. And you're to keep your cell phone on at all times. Understood?"

"Okay." Zane rolled his eyes at me and heaped some salad onto his plate.

"Good." Daddy cut off a bit of his steak and tossed it to Lucky. "Let's eat."

After supper I called Shyla, but I got her answering machine. I left her a long message about how desperately I needed to go shopping, with the start of high school only a couple of weeks away. "Besides," I said to her answering machine, "you haven't met Lucky yet. He's awesome."

For several days I heard nothing, but on Friday

afternoon Shyla pulled into the driveway, honked the horn, and yelled, "Anybody home?"

"Shyla!" I jumped into her arms and she whirled me around. Lucky ran out and started barking, demanding his fair share of attention.

"So, this is Lucky!" Shyla bent down and nuzzled his face. "He's even cuter than I imagined. What a doll! Does Mama know?"

"What do *you* think?"

Shyla laughed. "She'll have a fit when she finds out a dog is living under her roof."

"Zane says to cross that bridge when I get to it."

Shyla unlocked the car trunk and grabbed her duffel bag.

"That's all you brought?" I was so relieved to see her that I was fairly dancing up the porch steps.

"I have to go back to Austin on Sunday," Shyla said.

We went into the house. Lucky plopped down in the kitchen and pressed his belly to the cool floor. Shyla dropped her bag in the hallway and looked around. "Where's Zane?"

"Spending the night at Will's house. The swim team is throwing him a welcome-back-to-society party tomorrow."

"He finished his community service, then. Good for him."

"Like he had a choice."

"You'd be surprised how many people flout the law," Shyla said.

"Not when their daddy is a judge."

Shyla grinned. "I guess not. But I'm proud of Zane for sticking it out."

We went upstairs to Shyla's room. After Shyla left for college, Mama started using the closet to store her Bee Beautiful products, but otherwise the room remained a shrine to Shyla. Her bed, her dresser, and her bulletin board, crammed with photos, dried corsages, prom tickets, and theater programs, were just the way she'd left them. Shyla dropped her duffel on the bed and peered at herself in the mirror. "Gosh, I'm a mess."

But to me she looked perfect in a white shirt, tight jeans, and a brown leather belt that matched her sandals. She ran a comb through her hair and put on some more lipstick. "So. You want to go out to the mall?"

"Now?"

"Why not? The stores are open till ten. We'll let Daddy's office know where we are, and maybe we'll meet him later for dinner. Sound good?"

On the way to the mall I filled Shyla in on everything she'd missed since her last trip home at spring break. I told her about house-sitting for Beverly and about the presents she'd brought us from England: an expensive watch for Zane, leather-bound books for Daddy, the sweater for me, the bone for Lucky.

"Sounds like Beverly has really taken to the Trask family," Shyla said.

"It's weird. She barely knows us, and she's always buying us stuff. And the way she sucks up to Daddy makes me gag. Of course, you keep saying it's all my imagination, but it's not."

"Maybe she *is* trying too hard, but she's new in town, and her husband just died."

"He didn't *just* die. It's been two years. You'd think she'd be over it by now."

Shyla pulled into the turn lane for the mall. "She's probably lonely."

We parked near the main entrance and went into the mall. Shyla dropped her keys into her purse and propped her sunglasses on top of her head. "Where to first?"

"I need everything," I said.

We bought my gym stuff first, then headed for Dazzle, where I picked out a pair of distressed jeans and a skirt I'd seen in a magazine. "It looks pretty short, though."

"Let's see it on you," Shyla said.

She grabbed a couple of tops off the rack, and I went to the dressing room. As I put on the skirt, she tossed a plain white knit top over the top of the door. "Try this with it."

I pulled the top on and checked out the outfit in the three-way mirror.

"You're right," Shyla said. "Wear that skirt to school and you'll get arrested. The top is cool, though."

"It's boring."

"It's ladylike."

"I'm fourteen. I'm too young to be a lady."

Shyla laughed. "We'll spice it up with a jacket or something. Try the jeans."

While I got into the jeans, Shyla found a wide belt and a ruby-colored velvet jacket. Which I would never have thought of, but somehow it all worked.

"See?" Shyla said. "You look hip as all get-out. It's perfect."

Shyla handed over her credit card, and we left Dazzle and walked down a few doors to Ritzy Girls. Shyla led me past racks of stretchy tops, funky hats, and sequined skirts to a section of the store displaying more ordinary-looking stuff. She picked out pants, a sweater, and a khaki skirt that came all the way to my knees. She said it was a classic. To me it just looked boring.

"I look like a candidate for the rest home," I said when I came out to model the skirt and sweater. "Nobody at Eden High would be caught dead wearing this stuff."

"The confident girls will," Shyla said.

"But I'm not confident! I'm just praying I can find my locker and survive first-year algebra."

"Girls who dress like pop tarts are the ones who feel the least sure of themselves on the inside," Shyla said. "Besides, that skirt shows off your curves beautifully."

"What curves?" I muttered. But secretly I was pleased to get a compliment from Shyla the Magnificent. I changed back into my own clothes and came out of the dressing room with the new stuff draped over my arm. "I'll take the sweater and the pants. But ix-nay on the skirt."

Shyla put her arm around my shoulder and peered into my face. "Look at me, Phoebe. I know you're feeling pressure to get everything right, but freshman year is not as all-important as people think. Everybody in your class will be in the same boat. Insecure, afraid, and trying desperately not to show it. In the long run it won't matter whether you wear a red sweater or a blue one, or whether your jeans came from the right store. Be friendly with everyone, study hard, try something new, and you'll be fine."

"You make it sound easy."

"It *is* easy, I promise. Now, let's relax, have a good time, and max out the old credit card. Okay?"

By the time I bought shoes from Happy Feet, and two more pairs of jeans from the department store opposite the food court, we were starving and tired of dragging our shopping bags around, so we found a table and bought colas and soft pretzels to tide us over until dinnertime.

Shyla leaned back in her chair and sighed. "Man, this brings back so many memories of shopping with Mama. I still miss her like crazy."

"You're never home anyway."

"That's true. I guess I just felt safe knowing she was there if I needed her."

I ate a bite of pretzel. "All she cares about now is her Bee Beautiful stuff."

"I don't think that's entirely true," Shyla said. "But she's addicted to all the attention she's getting. It's hard for somebody like Mama to walk away when everybody is telling her how smart and wonderful she is."

"I don't get it."

"When she was young, Mama never got to stay in one place for very long. All through school she was the new kid, trying to fit in. But every time she made a friend, the army sent her dad someplace else and she had to start over." Shyla sipped her cola and rattled the ice in her cup. "Now she's the center of attention at Bee Beautiful, and it's hard to give it up."

I smeared mustard on the last bit of my pretzel and wondered why Shyla knew so much of our mother's history, while I didn't have a clue. I wanted to hear more. If I understood why Mama had chosen Bee Beautiful over me, maybe I could figure out how to deal. But before I could say anything else, a familiar voice said, "Phoebe? Is that you, darlin'?"

Beverly was standing beside our table, beaming down at us like we were the lost treasure of Atlantis.

"Hi, Beverly," I said.

My sister stood up. "You must be Beverly Grace. I'm Shyla Trask, Phoebe's sister."

"Oh, honey, don't get up!" Beverly waved Shyla back into her chair. "I recognize you from that charming portrait in your dining room, although I must say you're even prettier in person."

"Thank you."

I chewed my pretzel. Shyla said, "Would you care to join us?"

"I'd love to, but I've got to get home and finish some work. My trip put me behind schedule again, but I couldn't bear the thought of not being there when the university honored my husband. Marshall would have been pleased to see how many people showed up."

Shyla said, "You were married to Marshall Grace?"

"For nearly twelve years. We coauthored a couple of books on the Tudor age."

"I read them!" Shyla said, looking way more impressed than I wanted her to be. "Last year in my world history class."

"I hope they were helpful."

Beverly patted my shoulder. "I spoke with your daddy this morning. I invited you all to dinner tonight, and I'm disappointed you can't make it. But I do understand how pressed for time he must feel with that big trial coming up."

"Yeah, we're all pretty busy," I said. "We'll probably be busy for a really long time."

Shyla said, "It was nice meeting you, Mrs. Grace."

Beverly waved and headed for the escalator.

"Wow," Shyla said. "She's gorgeous."

"*Now* do you see why I'm worried?"

"Listen, Phoebe, you've got to stop obsessing about her and Dad. So they were in a car together one day. It doesn't mean anything. There could be all sorts of perfectly harmless reasons for it."

"Then, why wouldn't Dad admit he'd been out with her? Besides, it's way more than just that one day. It's the presents, and the way she says *ciao* and *presto* instead of speaking English, and the way she touches his arm every chance she gets, and the way she calls him 'Sum-nuh' in that slow-molasses Southern-belle voice, like it's 1860 and she's just stepped off her daddy's plantation."

Shyla chewed thoughtfully. "If you're worried about it, you should stay close with her. It'll be easier to keep track of what's going on until Mama gets home."

"Excuse me," I said. "Have you looked outside lately? Hell hasn't frozen over yet."

"Gosh, Phoebe," Shyla said. "When did you develop such a fresh mouth?"

"I don't know. Maybe it was when I practically became an orphan." I was about to cry, and I didn't want to have a major meltdown in the mall. I grabbed my shopping bags. "Can we go now?"

"Sure." Shyla glanced at her watch and opened her cell phone. "Let's call the judge and see where he wants to meet us for dinner. I'm still famished."

The following night Zane left for his big to-do at the lake, and Daddy took Shyla and me to Gus's for burgers and fries. All they could talk about was the big trial coming up, which bored me to tears. When we got home, I switched on the TV in the den and curled up with Lucky to watch a movie, but with the start of freshman year just a day away, I was too keyed up to concentrate. Around ten I gave up and went to bed, but I was still awake, tossing and turning in the dark, when Zane came home an hour later. I heard him say good night to Daddy and Shyla. Then he came upstairs, tapped our code on my door, and stuck his head in. "Are you awake?"

Lucky opened one eye, saw that it was Zane, and resumed his doggy dreams.

"I'm awake."

He came in and sprawled on my beanbag chair. "Butterflies in your stomach thinking about school?"

That was one of the best things about my big brother. He could always tell what I was feeling without my having to say anything.

"Shyla says it's no big deal."

"School was always a breeze for her."

"How was the party? Did you have a good time?"

"It was kind of a bust after Dad nixed the overnight thing. A couple of the guys never showed. Mostly it was just Ryan, Will, and me scarfing down pizza and talking. It sure feels good to have my car back, though."

"No kidding. I do not want to ride the bus to school. At least not at first."

"Don't worry, princess," Zane said. "Your chariot awaits."

"Some chariot. When are you going to get that bumper fixed?"

"As soon as I get ahold of some more cash. All my savings went to pay for those stupid mailboxes." Zane glanced at my shopping bags piled in the corner. "Looks like you don't have any cash flow problems, though. Did you get some neat stuff?"

"Yeah, but Beverly showed up at the food court. I nearly gagged on my pretzel."

"Man," Zane said. "That woman is on us like white on rice."

"Shyla thinks it's because Beverly is lonely."

"So is Dad. That's why they're a dangerous combination." Zane yawned and got to his feet. "I'm beat. I'm going to grab some z's."

At my door he stopped and turned around. "Don't worry about school, okay? You'll be fine."

The next morning, after Daddy's traditional Sunday pancake feast, Shyla gave me a manicure using Mama's newest Bee Beautiful polish, a shimmering color called Pink Diamonds. While we waited for the polish to dry, she went through my closet, organizing my new clothes to make it easier for me to put myself together.

"There," she said when my skirts, tops, jackets, and jeans were arranged to her satisfaction. "Now you won't have to dig around looking for stuff in the morning." She inspected my new manicure. "Looks good. Have you shaved your pits?"

"Shyla!"

She grinned. "Well, it's gonna be hotter than tamales tomorrow. You might want to wear something sleeveless, in which case you don't want to look like King Kong."

"I can't decide what to wear."

"All your stuff is cute. Just close your eyes and pick something." She got up. "I have to go. It's a long drive to Austin, and I'm working tonight. Jimmie Vaughan is playing. The place will be packed."

I went outside to see her off. She hugged Daddy, cracked a joke with Zane, and kissed Lucky. Then she held out her arms to me. I latched on to her, breathing in the smells of perfume and shampoo until she practically had to pry my hands away.

"Thanks for taking me shopping," I said.

"It was fun," Shyla said. "Good luck at school tomorrow."

"I'll need it."

"Just remember what I told you and you'll do great."

"I'll try."

"I'll call you tomorrow night after my shift is over, and you can give me all the details."

Daddy said, "Remember that we're screening our calls now, Shyla."

"I'm telling you, Dad," Shyla said, "you should just call the phone company and get caller ID."

"Maybe I will." He kissed her cheek. "Drive carefully. Keep your cell phone on."

Shyla put her sunglasses on and tossed her duffel bag in the trunk. She punched Zane on the arm. "Keep your nose clean, ace."

"Don't worry, I will."

She backed to the street, tooted the horn, and drove away. We went inside. Daddy spread his papers on the desk in the den and turned on his laptop. I helped Zane clear away the breakfast mess, then spent the afternoon in my room e-mailing Lauren and deciding what to wear for my first day at Eden High. Shyla had left a fashion magazine open to an article called "What's Your Style?" which showed different ways of putting yourself together based on the message you wanted to convey.

"What's your style?" the article began. "Fun and flirty? Sexy but serious? Cool and classy? Follow these hints to put together a look that will make you unforgettable, no matter which look you choose."

Cool and classy was the style Shyla had recommended for me, and I have to admit it looked really great in the magazine. I had the clothes to copy the look, but inside I felt more awkward and afraid than cool and classy.

The next morning I forced down a bowl of cereal and some OJ for breakfast and got dressed. By then Daddy had left for an early meeting at the courthouse, and Zane was waiting in the car, the radio cranked loud enough to wake the dead. When I slid into the front seat, he gave me a thumbs-up sign. "Say what you will about old Shyla, but she does have good taste. You look great, Phoebe."

"Thanks." It was way too hot to wear a jacket like in the magazine, and I'd had a hard time making up my mind. After changing clothes half a dozen times, I'd settled on a black skirt, a cotton top, and the silver and turquoise bracelets Mama had given me for Christmas last year.

Zane backed down the driveway, and we started the twenty-minute drive to Eden High. The school was fairly new, having opened when Shyla was a freshman. It was made of red brick, with plenty of long windows running across the front. A covered walkway connected the main buildings to the gym and the auditorium, where the freshmen had been told to report.

Zane pulled around a couple of buses idling in the driveway, wheeled into a parking space reserved for upperclassmen, and killed the engine. The lot was filling up fast; everybody was talking and laughing, full of first-day nerves. He grabbed his backpack off the backseat and opened his door. "Welcome to high school, kiddo," he said. "Knock 'em dead."

"Yeah, right."

He grinned. "I'll meet you here after school, okay?"

At the front entrance he pointed me toward the auditorium and jogged across the grass to hang with the swim team. Will and Ryan waved to me as I went inside. I looked around for a familiar face and spotted Katie Phelps and Gillian Palmer, who had both been in my homeroom last year. I didn't know them very well, but Katie had been on the eighth-grade cheerleading squad with Lauren. I waved to them, and Gillian waved back but went on talking to Katie. The seats in their row were taken anyway, so I moved on.

The auditorium buzzed with sound as students

from three different middle schools came in looking for seats. I found a spot on the center aisle and sat down, dropping my backpack onto the empty chair beside me. The lights flickered, like they do at a concert to tell you when intermission is over, and the school principal, Mrs. Cantrell, walked to the podium. "Good morning!"

She waited for conversations to stop, introduced herself, and welcomed us to Eden High.

Then a voice whispered in my ear, "Is that seat taken?"

A boy with deep blue eyes, a killer smile, and a shock of black hair was standing there looking down at me. I grabbed my stuff off the chair and scooted over, and he sat down. "Thanks."

Mrs. Cantrell was going over the school district's rules of conduct, as if we hadn't had them drilled into our brains for eight years running. She asked us to take out our class schedules. Papers rustled. Somebody giggled. Somebody else coughed. The boy leaned toward me to take his folded-up paper out of his pocket. He smelled great. Like soap and spearmint gum. He unfolded his paper as Mrs. Cantrell, silhouetted in the light of an overhead projector, slid a floor plan of the school onto the projector and adjusted the image on the screen behind her. She pointed out the locations of the library, the cafeteria, the gym, the rest rooms, and the science labs.

We followed along, figuring out how to get from English to algebra to science to lunch before the tardy bells rang.

Then the back doors of the auditorium opened, and the band marched down the aisles playing the school song. The cheerleaders ran onto the stage, clapping and yelling. The head cheerleader grabbed the microphone off the podium and strode to the center of the stage, her white skirt swirling around her perfectly tanned legs.

"Are y'all ready to learn a cheer?" she yelled.

The boy beside me rolled his eyes, which made me like him right away, since I am not much of a rah-rah type person myself. My theory on school is get in, do the work, get out.

"Okay, y'all!" the cheerleader yelled. "We're gonna learn a cheer called 'Blue and White.' This is the one we'll start with at all our pep rallies this season. Learn it now and be ready to cheer for the Eagles at our rally on Friday. First of all"—she strode to the right side of the stage—"this side of the room is the blue side. And this side"—she motioned to the left—"is the white side."

Behind her seven cheerleader clones lined up and clapped their hands. "Ready-o? Let's go! It's a blue, it's a blue, it's a blue, blue, blue!"

They pivoted left. "It's a white, it's a white, it's a white, white, white!

"It's a blue!

"It's a white!

"Blue! White! Fight, fight, fight!"

After we practiced yelling for the good old blue and white, the band played another song, and Mrs. Cantrell finally turned us loose. The boy beside me stood up. I remembered Shyla's advice to be friendly to everybody, but before I could say anything, he disappeared into the crowd of people standing in the aisle. I headed for French One, my first-period class, where the teacher, Elise Hartwell Rochard, who had been only a couple of years ahead of Shyla in school, informed us that from that day forward she would be Madame Rochard and would respond to us only in French. Plus we would be graded not only on our written homework and class participation, but on the authenticity of our accents during a spring dinner to be held at L'Antibes. Imagine me attempting to pronounce *moules à la béarnais* or *tarte au citron* correctly and you can understand why I had no hope of getting an A in French.

From Madame's class it was on to English lit, algebra, and finally lunch. I bought two slices of cheese pizza and a soda and took my tray outside. The cheerleaders were running around acting as social directors, finding seats for everybody, making sure nobody was left to eat alone. One of them directed me to a table where two other girls, both blondes, had just sat down.

Right away I could tell that they were best friends. They wore the same nail polish and lipstick, and they'd color-coordinated their clothes for the all-important first day. Even though Shyla said it was dumb to try to look like a clone of somebody else, and that dressing like twins only showed a lack of imagination, I wished all over again that Lauren hadn't moved away.

Blonde number one said, "Hi. I'm Ashley, and this is Courtney. We went to West Middle School."

"I'm Phoebe." I popped open my soda can and stuck a straw into the opening. "I went to Eden Middle School."

"Oh, that old building near downtown," Courtney said. "My mom used to teach there. She loved it."

Courtney bit into her burger, but Ashley pushed her tuna sandwich aside. "I'm too stressed to eat. I can't wait for this day to be over."

"Me either," Courtney said. "Mom says the first day is the worst, though. She says high school will get easier once we learn the routine."

"I hope so." I took a bite of pizza just as the boy from the auditorium passed our table. He was talking to a couple of other guys as a cheerleader guided them to a table under the trees, but when he saw me, he raised his hand and nodded.

"He's really cute," Courtney said. "What's his name?"

"I don't know. He sat beside me at the assembly."

"And you let him get away?" Ashley twisted around for a better look. "I *know* he didn't go to West. I would have noticed."

"Hey, look," Courtney said, tucking a strand of hair behind her ear. "There's Madame Rochard."

Our French teacher was standing near the door gnawing on a drumstick and talking to Mrs. Cantrell.

"You have her too?" I asked.

Courtney nodded. "Second period. She's gonna be a major pain."

Ashley grinned at her friend. "Who did you get for world history?"

"Don't know yet. I have it next period."

"Me too," I said, relieved that I would know at least one person in the class.

We compared our schedules and discovered that all three of us would have PE together seventh period. "Thank God," Ashley said. "Going into PE alone is the absolute worst kind of torture."

"Whoever gets to the gym first, save places on the bleachers, okay?" Courtney said. "I hate sitting on the floor."

The bell rang and we scattered. Ashley headed to English lit, Courtney and I to world history. The teacher, Mr. Clifton, handed out a five-page time line that included every event that had ever happened anywhere in the known universe, and spoke in a stupefied, gravelly monotone that put half the class to sleep. He explained that this year we would be reading about Goths and Visigoths, Byzantium and ancient Rome, Hitler and Attila the Hun and Mother Teresa. "In short," he intoned, "the en-tire glor-i-ous tap-es-try of hu-man his-to-ry."

Courtney opened her notebook and started drawing cartoon characters and writing captions in the bubbles above their heads. I tried to pay attention to Mr. Clifton, but I just couldn't work up any enthusiasm for that glorious tapestry he was talking about. My new sandals were pinching my feet and my head felt like it was about to explode. I glanced at the clock above the chalkboard. It seemed the day should be over by now, but it was only 1:25 and I still had science and PE to go.

At last the class ended. I said bye to Courtney and headed down the main hall, past the glass trophy cases and the administration offices, to the science lab and slid into a seat just as the bell rang.

The teacher, Mrs. Grady, had taught science at Eden High since the dawn of creation. I remembered her name because she was the only teacher who had ever accused my sister of not working up to her potential, all because Shyla was one day late turning in some dumb experiment. Mrs. Grady did not care one iota that Shyla was late because she had to go to Austin to accept an academic award from the Texas governor. Rules were rules, and Shyla would not get an A in chemistry even though she'd aced all the tests. Daddy was furious and complained to the school board, but Shyla had already been accepted to every college to which she'd applied; what did she care about some rinky-dink high school science experiment?

As Mrs. Grady began going over her rules, I looked around the room for a familiar face, and there he was. The boy from the auditorium, sitting three rows away, perusing his textbook. I couldn't explain why looking at him gave me such a fluttering feeling in the pit of my stomach. I'd met tons of Zane's friends, cute guys from the swim team who hung out at our house or at the lake. None of them affected me like this blue-eyed stranger. When Mrs. Grady called the roll, I learned that his name was Nick Harper.

Mrs. Grady handed out the reading assignments for the first semester and assigned us to our lab partners. Miraculously, I was paired with Nick.

"You're Phoebe, right?" he asked after Mrs. Grady had told us to rearrange our chairs in pairs. "You're the girl from the auditorium."

"Right." My heart was racing. Stupid.

We filled out a worksheet, matching a set of vocabulary words to their definitions. With Nick looking up stuff in the glossary and me filling in the blanks, we powered through the list in no time, crossing off the words as we went: "magma," "opsonin," "rhizoid." While we waited for the others to finish, Nick told me he'd moved to Eden from Houston because his dad got a new job at the electric company. His mom had been a nurse, but now she was staying home to take care of his little brother, Jacob. Like me, he had an older sister who was away at school.

When it was my turn to talk, I told him my dad was a judge, my brother was a junior and on the swim team, and my sister was studying for law school at UT.

"Wow," Nick said. "You have a lot to live up to."

"Yeah, but my dad is pretty cool about it. He doesn't pressure me or anything."

"What about your mom?"

I toyed with my pen. "I don't see her much. She's the national spokeswoman for Bee Beautiful cosmetics. She travels a lot."

Mrs. Grady rapped on her desk. "Ten more minutes, people. Hurry up and finish."

Nick said, "Man, that's tough. When I was a kid, my dad traveled for a while. Every time he called home, my mom cried."

"My mom will be coming home soon, though. For good."

I hoped that saying it aloud would somehow make it so.

Mrs. Grady came around to collect our papers.

When the bell rang, Nick slid out of his seat and scooped up his books. "See you."

I don't even remember going to PE that day. Later Courtney told me that I came into the gym looking dazed, like I'd just survived a major earthquake. That's how much Nick Harper had rocked my world.

After PE, I met Zane in the parking lot, and he talked all the way home. His classes were okay. The coach hadn't mentioned the incident with the mailboxes and the graffiti, and his first team meeting had been a blast. But the best part was that Ginger Threadgill was in his American history class.

Then I told him about Madame Rochard and about having lunch with Ashley and Courtney. But I didn't tell my brother about my lab partner. I didn't even tell Shyla when she called home late that night to see how my first day of high school had turned out. Nick Harper was a wonderful secret I wanted all to myself.

A couple of weeks into the year Mrs. Cantrell announced that the traditional freshman shindig known as the Howdy Dance would be held a week from Saturday. It wasn't really a dating event; people were supposed to mingle, eat pizza, and be home by 11 p.m.

"It's fun," Zane said when I told him about it on the way home from school that afternoon. "Even though hardly anybody dances. It's pretty much boys on one side of the room, girls on the other. Still, you should go."

We passed the fried-chicken place on the highway, and the smell of sizzling drumsticks wafted through the open car windows. My stomach rumbled. I'd waited after school for Zane to finish swim practice because the flag burners' trial had opened that week. We hadn't had any more hang-up calls, but Daddy didn't want either of us to be home alone. Now it was almost suppertime and I was famished.

"Ashley and Courtney are going," I said. "We were

talking about what to wear at lunch today. Ashley's going to ask her mom to take us shopping."

"Great." Zane braked for the stop light across from the courthouse. "Just don't max out Dad's credit cards. *I* need new stuff once in a while."

I glanced up at the second-floor windows in Daddy's courtroom. The protesters had chosen to have a judge hear their case instead of a jury, and Daddy was hoping to wrap it up quickly. A TV news crew camped at the courthouse every day, waiting for Daddy's decision. Today a young blond reporter in a red suit and black stilettos was standing on the courthouse steps sipping a can of cola and talking to her cameraman.

"Maybe the trial will be over today," I said as the light changed and we drove past.

"The newspapers say the lawyers are calling so many witnesses it'll go on until Halloween at least."

"I wish the papers would get off Daddy's back about it. It's not like he can send those guys to jail just because the town doesn't like what they did."

"It's more than burning the flag and setting the fire," Zane said. "People are mad because the protesters endangered everybody when that gun went off. It was lucky nobody got shot, or trampled trying to get away."

"It *was* dangerous," I said. "But nobody got hurt. Can you put someone in jail for scaring people?"

"They'll do time for setting the fire at the courthouse," Zane said. "I hope that'll be enough to satisfy the rednecks around here."

The light changed to green, but instead of turning toward home, Zane headed out toward the Dallas highway. "How about an early supper at Gus's? There's no telling when the judge will get home, and I'm starved."

"Okay." I pulled the sun visor down to shade my eyes. "I just hope this whole trial thing is over soon."

Zane took his eyes off the road long enough to look at me. "Don't let the gossip get to you, Phoebe."

"How did you know?" I hadn't told anybody about the conversation I'd overheard on the day the trial opened. I was hurrying to get from my locker on the third floor to Mr. Clifton's class when I heard a couple of boys accusing Daddy of being a traitor for not throwing the book at the flag-burning cowards, no matter what the law said. "A real patriot would find a way to make them pay," one of them said. "Judge Trask is hiding behind this equal protection crap because he's too chicken to stand up for the flag."

Now Zane said, "I hear what they're saying at school about Dad too. They're judging him before the trial is over. A couple of guys on the team rag on Dad when they think I'm not listening. Even my history teacher mentioned the trial in class last week."

He pulled into the parking lot at Gus's, which was

packed even though it was early. "We can't let them get to us, Phoebe."

"That's what Mama said on the phone last night when I told her about that newspaper article."

"Well, for once I agree with her. We just have to hold our heads up until the trial is over. Let's go."

We went inside. People were standing three deep around the counter, shouting orders at Gus, who was flipping burgers as fast as he could. The whole place smelled wonderfully of hamburger meat and hot french fries.

"It'll be an hour before we get a table," Zane said, looking around the room. "Let's get the burgers to go."

He gave Gus our order, and half an hour later we were home. We pulled into the garage just as Beverly was leaving. She tooted her horn and waved as she drove away.

We went inside. Zane got a couple of plates out of the cabinet. I poured some iced tea and got the ketchup out of the fridge, and we sat down to our feast. While we ate, Zane told me about the swim meet coming up on Saturday and about how one of the boys on the other team was a contender for the next Olympics. "He'll be tough to beat," Zane said. "I just hope he doesn't embarrass me too bad in front of Ginger."

"Ginger's going?" I added more salt to my fries.

"That's great! Her dad finally let you off the hook, huh?"

"Not exactly. He still won't let us go out by ourselves, but he's letting her go to the meet with some of her friends."

"That's better than nothing."

"Yeah." Zane grinned. "I'm hoping he'll let us go to a Halloween costume party next month. Ginger says some of the customers at the garage have been working on Mr. Threadgill, telling him what a great guy I am, softening him up."

He punched the remote on the TV and flipped through the sports channels while we finished our burgers. I thought about how Zane had always been the one living on the edges of our family, but he seemed to have more close friends than either Shyla or me.

Since the school year started, I'd developed a tentative friendship with Courtney and Ashley; we hung out at lunch and made sure we chose one another when teams were formed in PE. Courtney had borrowed my homework one day, and Ashley loaned me a dollar when the snack machine ate all my money, but we weren't yet to the stage of calling one another on a regular basis, of sharing our innermost thoughts and feelings. They were still each other's best friend; I was just a tagalong.

As for Nick Harper, he was Mystery Man. He acted

like he liked me; he was always nice to me during science class, setting out all our equipment for experiments and letting me go first when we had to look into the microscope. The first time I wore the jeans I'd bought at Dazzle, he told me I looked great, but outside of class I ceased to exist. I wanted him to know I liked him, but I didn't know how to tell him. What if I risked saying something and he totally rejected me? I'd still be stuck with him as a lab partner, and it would be just too awkward.

Zane took his plate to the sink, ran some water over it, and said, "See you. I've got homework."

I had homework too, but I wasn't ready to tackle it yet. I flipped through the channels, but there was nothing to watch. I checked out the Beauty Channel. A woman with vampire nails was selling a ponytail wig that you could wear a whole bunch of different ways. She claimed the Pony Partner would make anybody look instantly elegant, but the models were so pretty they'd have looked great even if somebody had snatched them bald-headed.

I had just switched off the TV when our front window shattered, sending glass flying everywhere. I screamed. Outside car tires squealed.

Zane raced down the stairs. "What happened?"

"Somebody just broke our window!" I yelled.

Zane grabbed the phone. "I'm calling the courthouse."

A rock the size of a softball was lying on the floor. Wrapped around it was a piece of notebook paper held in place by a rubber band.

"Don't touch it!" Zane said. "It might have fingerprints. Damn! Dad's office isn't picking up."

"Maybe he's already on the way home," I said. "Call 911."

Zane punched in the emergency number. Five minutes later a police car pulled up to the house, at about the same time Dad arrived.

"Zane! Phoebe!" Daddy yelled, charging into the house. "Are you all right?"

The policeman followed Daddy inside and bent over the rock. "There's writing on this paper."

He put on some rubber gloves and gingerly unwrapped the rock.

"'Bena-dick Arnold,'" Dad read. "Well," he said grimly, "we know one thing about whoever did this: They can't spell Benedict correctly."

The cop turned to me and Zane. "Did either of you see anything?"

I told him I'd heard tires squealing but that everything had happened too fast.

He dropped the rock into a brown evidence bag and wrote up a report. Dad swept up the glass, and he and Zane boarded up the broken window. The police chief himself came out to the house, and he and Daddy talked outside on the porch. I desperately wanted to call Mama and Shyla so they could tell me not to freak, that everything would be okay, but Mama was on an airplane headed for Los Angeles, and Shyla was still on her shift at Jazz-n-Java. Daddy said there was no sense worrying them right then, when there was nothing either of them could do anyway. "We'll call tomorrow," he said, "when we're calmer and we have more details."

The police chief sent a patrol car to watch our house. We finally got to bed around midnight, but I lay wide awake in the dark, too unnerved to sleep. Maybe I should have been most concerned about the people threatening us, but the number one thing I worried about was whether Ashley and Courtney would still be friends with me when they found out what had happened. People in Eden are funny. They're quick to help you if you need a jump start for your car battery on a cold morning or an emergency babysitter for your kids, but they turn away at the first hint of real trouble, like they're afraid it might be contagious. And I wondered what Nick would think about a girl who needed police protection.

By the time Zane and I pulled into the student parking lot the next morning, the news had spread all over the place. The swim team surrounded our car and started peppering Zane with questions before we could even get the doors open.

"What happened?"

"Did you see who did it?"

"Are you okay, man?" Will asked when we finally got out of the car.

"I'm fine." Zane ducked his head, clearly embarrassed by all the attention. He grabbed his stuff off the backseat and locked the car.

We started for the front door with our entourage in tow. Ashley came running up to me, her china blue eyes big as saucers. "Omigod, Phoebe, I heard about what happened last night. Are you hurt or anything?"

"I'm okay."

She fell into step beside us. "Gosh, I never met anyone who was actually the target of a death threat before."

"It wasn't a death threat," Zane said. "Just some bum trying to make a point about the trial."

He and Will headed for their first class. Ashley and I climbed the stairs to our lockers on the third floor. "Listen, Phoebe, no offense or anything, okay?" she said. "I mean, I think you're great, but my dad says I should stay away from you until this trouble blows over."

I spun the combination and opened my locker, pretending to search for something inside, hiding my tears. Even though her reaction was pretty much what I'd expected, it still hurt. And if Ash wasn't allowed to hang out with me, neither would Courtney. I'd be alone at lunch, a reject. I couldn't go shopping with them for the Howdy Dance either.

Even though it was totally irrational, I was furious with Daddy. If he'd never become a judge, none of this would have happened. Mama wouldn't have felt the need to run away and prove herself, and I could have had a normal high school life. I dug my French text out of my locker and pasted a smile on my face. "Sure," I said to Ashley. "No problem."

"Great! I knew you'd understand. And when all this is over . . ." Her voice trailed away. The bell rang. Ashley grabbed her books. "See ya!"

I headed to French class, where Madame Rochard obviously thought the best way to deal with my situation was to keep me busy. She called on me three times—twice during the vocabulary drill and once in the conversation practice, which was a totally stupid exchange between two people who took turns astutely observing that the sky was blue.

For the rest of the morning, rumors flew around my head like a swarm of locusts as people shared what they'd heard and added their own embellishments: The rock throwing was an attempt to get back at Zane for damaging the mailboxes; it was a death threat against my whole family from the Mafia; I had been hit in the head and taken to the hospital in a coma.

The teachers patted my shoulder and smiled at me till their faces must have hurt. A few people whispered as I walked past. Others stared in a kind of morbid fascination, the way people gawk at a train wreck. It made me feel weird, but at the same time I could understand it. When a rock came flying through the judge's front window in the middle of a trial, it was big news.

At lunch I took my tray outside. The table where Ash and Courtney sat was completely full; they smiled sheepishly when I went past. At the far end of the courtyard I found an empty table. I wiped it off with an extra napkin, sat down, and unwrapped my sandwich.

"Hey, is this seat taken?"

"Nick!"

He slid into the chair across from me and brushed a lock of hair out of his eyes. "Weird morning?"

"It's pretty strange." Also pretty strange: My lab partner had decided to acknowledge my presence on the planet outside the science classroom. Not that I was complaining.

He stuck a straw into his soda can. "Were you scared?"

"Not at first. It happened too fast. Then my dad came home. The cops came. A patrol car spent the night outside our house."

"I heard."

"I got scared thinking about what could have happened." I munched on a potato chip and told Nick about the hang-up calls, which had stopped as abruptly as they'd started.

Nick chewed thoughtfully. "Whoever is doing this

would have to be incredibly stupid to try anything else now that the police are watching. It'll be okay. You just have to hang tough until the trial is over."

"That's weeks away," I said. "A long time to worry about it."

"You're fourteen. Let the grown-ups worry." Nick picked up his tray. "Gotta go. See you in class."

After school that day Zane dropped me at home because he had a dentist appointment. Daddy planned to adjourn court early so he could be at home with me, even though a police car was still parked across the street. The cop was reading a paperback book and sipping coffee from a Styrofoam cup. He looked up and nodded as I unlocked the front door.

The window repair people had already worked their magic. The house looked normal, as if nothing at all had happened. I dropped my books on the coffee table and went to the fridge for a soda. Five minutes later Beverly came over and gave me a bear hug, nearly spilling my cola. "Phoebe, darlin', I am so sorry about this trouble. Are you all right?"

To my horror, tears welled in my eyes. I blinked them away. "I'm okay."

"Your daddy's been delayed at the courthouse. He asked if I'd come over and stay with you until he gets here. He doesn't want you to be alone."

"There's a cop with a gun out front. I'm pretty safe."

"I know, but he still worries. All parents do."

I sipped my soda. The clock in Daddy's den ticked loudly into the silence. Beverly said, "You can be so careful, warning your children every minute of some danger, and still they can be taken from you in a split second."

Then I remembered the photo of the little boy I'd seen in her office.

"I had a son," Beverly said, as if she'd read my mind. "He drowned while we were on vacation at a beach resort south of Rome. He'd just turned nine."

"That's horrible!"

"Yes. It is. Marshall never got over it. And then I lost him, too."

Tears rolled down her face. I was shocked, and unsure of what you were supposed to do when a grown-up broke down right in front of you. I got her a tissue from the bathroom.

Beverly dabbed her eyes. "I'm sorry. You'd think I'd be over it by now."

But even I knew that some things were never over, no matter how bad you wanted them to be. I could see now that Beverly was trying so hard to be a part of our family in order to make up for the parts of hers that were lost forever.

"Listen," I said. "You want to sit down? You want a soda or something?"

"A soda would be nice." She sat down on the sofa while I went to the fridge. "Tell me about school."

I told her about Madame Rochard's impossible

standards in French One and about the boy who had slipped into a boredom-induced coma in Mr. Clifton's class and ended up in the hospital with seven stitches in his head where it had hit the floor when he fell.

"Everybody has had at least one teacher like your Mr. Clifton," Beverly said. "I once had a math professor who spoke with his back to the class for the entire semester and mumbled so badly we had to guess at what he was saying."

"Teachers like that ought to come with a warning label."

She laughed. "Your daddy mentioned there's a dance coming up?"

"It's no big deal. I probably won't even go."

"You don't want to skip your first high school dance. If you do, you'll look back in ten years and regret it."

She set her soda can on the leather coaster Daddy used when he was watching football on TV. "Did you get anything to wear to the dance when your sister took you shopping?"

I'm not a judge's daughter for nothing. I could see from a mile away where she was headed with this line of questioning. "I'm sure I've got something that will do."

Beverly shook her head. "Not good enough. We need something to make those freshman boys forget all about football and video games."

She jumped up, all smiles again now that she had a new project. "Tomorrow's Saturday, and I haven't been shopping for ages. Let's drive up to Dallas. We'll make a day of it. What do you say?"

Maybe I felt sorry for her. Maybe I was just tired of everything going on in Eden and needed a change of scenery. Maybe in the back of my mind I was remembering Shyla's advice to keep my enemy close.

"Sure," I said. "Why not?"

Chapter Eleven

During our foray into the Dallas shopping scene I found out that not only was Beverly an accomplished writer, she was also a photographer whose work had been published in a bunch of famous magazines. Oh, and her paintings had been exhibited in galleries in California, New York, and several places in between. There was nothing she couldn't do. Mama was pretty and smart too, but compared to Beverly she was just a saleslady. I could see how the judge would be dazzled by such a potent combination of beauty and brains.

On the drive up we listened to CDs and talked about work and school and the haunted house the Rotary Club sponsored in Eden every year. I had loved it when I was a kid, but lately my life had become scary enough without seeking out a chance to be frightened. Besides, Eden High was sponsoring a carnival with food and a live band.

"I might check it out," I told Beverly as the scenery slid by and a blues song poured from the CD player. “Zane is going with some friends to a costume party.”

We were nearing Dallas, and Beverly sped up to merge onto the freeway. I sorted through her CD collection stashed in the car’s console. There was a bit of everything—hard rock, blues, jazz, country, even an ancient bluegrass album by Jimmy Bowers and the Bluegrass Boys with vocals by Melanie McClain.

Beverly saw me looking at it and said, “That one’s a real oldie from way back in the sixties. Marshall bought it when it first came out on CD. I’d forgotten it was in there.”

We pulled into the parking garage at the Galleria, took the elevator to the third floor, and crossed the gray-carpeted hallway into the mall. The stores were decorated with gold and orange leaves, pumpkins, and spice-scented candles. We checked out a couple of department stores, but I didn’t see anything I liked. In a small shop down from Saks, I found a suede skirt and jacket that were stylish but within the Eden High dress code.

“It’s perfect with your coloring,” Beverly said. “Try it on.”

While I was in the dressing room, Beverly found a pair of silver earrings and some patterned hose to finish off my outfit. I paid for everything with Daddy’s credit card and tagged along while Beverly bought a couple of skirts, a sweater, some French perfume, and two pairs of designer jeans. We took the escalator to the lower level and ate a late lunch at a table by the skating rink before starting for home.

On the drive back, Beverly hardly spoke. Maybe she was bored after spending all day with a high school student, or maybe she was thinking about her family. I couldn't help feeling sorry for her. I mean, how could a person go on living after her whole family had been wiped out? Even though I couldn't totally forgive her for the way she'd taken over our lives, I was mature enough to understand that when she looked at Daddy and Zane, she saw the ones who were lost to her forever.

As we left the interstate and headed down the Eden highway, Beverly turned on the radio and listened to a talk show on NPR. While the commentators were talking about events in Iraq, I gazed out the window and thought about the dance. I was nervous about going, especially with the trial still dragging on, but I was also excited, hoping I'd see Nick. Maybe we'd talk and he'd ask me to dance, and—

"Phoebe?" Beverly's voice interrupted my little fantasy. "Isn't that your brother's car?"

Zane was parked on the side of the road, near the spot where we'd rescued Lucky. As we got closer, he waved his arms to flag us down. Beverly pulled off the highway and lowered the car window. "Car trouble, Zane? Do you need a ride?"

Zane stuck his head into the car. "The trial's over."

"But it's Saturday!" I said.

"The lawyers called Dad this morning right after you left and said both sides were ready to make a deal. He went down to the courthouse, and they worked it all out. The protesters pled guilty to everything in exchange for a reduced sentence. Dad gave them three years in prison for arson, plus a fine and five years' probation." Zane ran his fingers through his hair. "It's a zoo downtown, Phoebe. People are swarming all over the courthouse. You didn't answer your cell phone, so Dad sent me out here to find you. He wants us to wait for him at Will's house until things calm down."

I got out of the car.

Beverly pushed her sunglasses to the top of her head. "I'll hang on to your new stuff, Phoebe, and keep an eye on your house until you all get home."

"Thanks. And thanks for taking me shopping."

"You're welcome. I enjoyed it."

We got into Zane's car. Beverly pulled around us and went on toward town. Zane made a U-turn and headed back out to the Hartes' house.

"Man," Zane said, "I am so glad this whole thing is over."

"I *hope* it's over," I said. "But it sounds like people are still really mad."

"A few rednecks are bent out of shape because the

protesters won't serve any time for burning the flag."

"But Daddy didn't have a choice! The law—"

"I know. But a couple of people stuck their faces into the TV camera and criticized him anyway, accusing him of being soft on crime." Zane slowed for a battered pickup pulling a bass boat. "You should have heard the speech the judge made to the press just now. He said the law is supposed to preserve and enlarge freedom, and that people's feelings about the flag don't outweigh the right to free speech, even when other people find such speech distasteful. Honest, Phoebe, the old judge sounded almost poetic."

We pulled into the Hartes' driveway, and Will and his dad came out. "Are you kids all right?" Mr. Harte asked.

"We're fine," Zane said, unfastening his seat belt.

"Come on in and make yourselves at home. My wife is at her garden club meeting, but she left some tea and sandwiches."

We went in. Mr. Harte made a beeline for the den, where the TV was blaring. Will's sister, Caroline, in denim cutoffs and a pink tank top, was in the kitchen putting ice into some glasses. "Hi, Phoebe," she said. "Are you okay?"

"Yeah. I missed all the excitement. I was shopping in Dallas."

"Lucky you! The stores around here haven't gotten in any new stuff in ages."

Will rolled his eyes at Zane. "Girl talk. Let's grab some food and split. The Rangers are on TV."

They loaded their plates and disappeared into the den. Caroline and I sat at the counter in the kitchen. She tore the crust off her sandwich and popped it into her mouth. "So, where'd you go shopping?"

"Galleria."

"Wow, I love that place! Did Shyla take you?"

"No. Our neighbor Beverly Grace."

"That writer lady? I saw her downtown the other day. She's so elegant, even in jeans." Caroline sipped her tea. "What all did you buy?"

"Just a skirt and jacket for the Howdy Dance." I described the outfit and the accessories I'd gotten to go with it.

"Sounds perfect," Caroline said. "My freshman year Mrs. Cantrell sent three girls home from the dance because their skirts were too short. When they bent over, you could see everything!"

"The judge would never let me out of the house looking like that." I crunched a handful of chips. "He's pretty strict."

Caroline nibbled her sandwich. "Is there somebody special you're seeing at the dance?"

I hadn't told Mama or Shyla or Zane about Nick, but for some reason I told Caroline everything—how we'd met on the first day of school and how he'd told me I looked good in my distressed jeans and how he'd sat with me at lunch after Ash and Courtney bailed on me. "He acts like he likes me, but he hasn't said anything directly, you know what I mean?"

"Boy, do I ever." Caroline added more sugar to her tea and stirred. "My boyfriend, Grady? It took him an entire year to ask me out, even though I was practically following him around with my tongue hanging out, dropping hints all over the place."

"Are guys really that clueless?"

Caroline laughed. "Who knows? But it sounds like Nick really likes you."

"How can I tell for sure?"

"If he keeps paying you compliments, sitting with you at lunch, that's a pretty good sign. It just takes time to get past that horrible, awkward getting-to-know-you stage." Caroline got a bunch of grapes from the fridge, washed them off at the sink, and set them on a plate. "If you see him at the dance, go over and say hello. Ask him what he thinks of the decorations, how he likes the music they're playing, whatever. But don't crowd him. If he thinks you're pushing him, he'll disappear faster than ice in August." She sipped more tea. "Always have your next move in mind."

"Next move?" I hadn't realized that simply showing up at a dance involved developing a strategy as complicated as the D-day invasion.

Caroline nodded. "After your conversation about

the music or the fake pumpkins or whatever, maybe he'll ask you to dance. If so, great. But if he doesn't, just say, 'See you later,' and move on, like there's someplace important you have to be. It's better if you can have a friend stationed nearby, but if not, head for the rest room. Don't run like you *have* to go or anything; just don't let Nick see you wandering around like a lost puppy."

"Yo, Caro!" Will hollered from the den. "Your favorite movie is coming on."

"*Casablanca*?" Caroline grabbed her plate and said to me, "You like Bogart?"

"He's okay."

"You *have* to see this movie. It's the best love story ever."

We took our food into the den and settled down to watch the movie, and like Caroline said, it was pretty romantic. Rick Blaine and Ilsa Lund fell in love in Paris and planned to run away together before the Nazis got there. But the day they were supposed to leave, Ilsa stood Rick up. He was so upset he moved to Casablanca and opened up a nightclub. One night Ilsa walked in with her long-lost husband, whom she thought was dead, throwing everybody's emotions into total chaos. It was a huge mess. Near the end Daddy came in, his shirt torn and bloodied, an angry welt on his cheek.

"Daddy, what happened?" I cried.

"Dad?" Zane said, coming to his feet. "Did you get into a fight?"

"I got caught between a couple of protesters and the TV guys, and a camera hit me in the face. Bloodied my nose."

Mr. Harte said, "Do you need a bandage, Judge? Some ice?"

"No, I'm fine. I've come to take my kids home. I appreciate your letting them stay here. Some folks in town wouldn't have been so welcoming, given the circumstances."

"Some folks are just plain ignorant," Mr. Harte said.

We left Rick and Ilsa standing on the tarmac at the airport in Casablanca, breaking up for good. Zane jumped into his car and took off. I got into Daddy's car. Caroline bent down and stuck her head though the open window and whispered, "Good luck with Nick, Phoebe."

When we got home, Daddy changed his shirt and got some ice for his bruised face. Later, over cups of cocoa and apple pie from the bakery downtown, he told Zane and me that most people understood he'd had to follow the law, but that didn't make his decision any easier to take.

"Some people may make disparaging remarks about me for a while," he warned. "And I'm sorry for that. But I'm not sorry for upholding the law."

Okay, I knew he was sworn to defend the Constitution and blah, blah, blah, but still, I was upset that he had made other people mad and that Zane and I probably hadn't heard the last of the gossip at school.

Lying in bed later that night, I put the whole trial episode out of my mind and thought about Caroline's strategy for dealing with Nick. He was hard to figure out, the way he acted so sweet one minute and wary the next, like he didn't want me to get too close. It drove me crazy. Still, when I was around Nick, it was easier to forget my problems and pretend that my family was whole and totally normal. I hoped he would ask me to dance. And I hoped that now Ashley and Courtney would lift their moratorium on contact with me and serve as my backup if he didn't.

The next morning, after Daddy made pancakes, he called Shyla and they discussed the trial in excruciating detail, even though she'd already heard about it on TV. Then Mama called home. After Daddy told *her* about the trial and Zane updated her on his life, I told her I was going to the Howdy Dance.

"I'm so disappointed I won't be there for that," Mama said.

"It's no big deal. All the freshmen are invited."

"I remember the year Shyla went," Mama said, her laughter bubbling up. "The way she agonized over which boys she wanted to dance with nearly drove me crazy. She reminded me of Scarlett O'Hara choosing a beau for the barbecue at Twelve Oaks. Finally I told her to stop obsessing or I'd make her stay home."

"I bet that got her attention," I said, thinking of how much my sister loved having a good time. Her motto was "Work hard, play hard."

"Tell me," Mama said. "What are you wearing to the dance?"

I described the skirt and jacket, but I didn't tell her how I'd gotten them. I'd already tried making Mama jealous by playing the Beverly card, and it hadn't worked. I didn't beg her to come back, either. It was obvious that she'd come home when she got good and ready, and there was nothing I could say that would hurry her along.

Mama said, "You be sure and have Daddy take your picture, honey."

Preserving my fourteen-year-old self on film had never been such a big deal to me, but because it was important to Mama, I promised.

Then she said, "If everything works out as planned, I'll be there next February to take pictures myself."

For a minute I couldn't believe my ears. I was afraid to hope. "You're coming home?" I asked.

The sound of her laugh settled over me like a warm blanket. "I told you I never planned to stay away forever. By February, I'll have reached all my goals, and my replacement will be ready to step into my role. By then I'll be ready to let someone else worry about the sales figures."

I let out a yelp that brought Zane and Daddy running. "Does Daddy know?"

"Do I know what?" Daddy asked.

"Mama's coming home!"

Zane said, "You're kidding me, right?"

I handed him the phone. "Ask her yourself if you don't believe me."

While Zane talked to Mama, Daddy told me that he and Mama had discussed the possibility of her coming home in the winter, but he hadn't wanted to tell us until she was sure. I wasn't the least bit surprised. Keeping secrets was the Trask way, but in this case I didn't care. The main thing was that our family was about to be put back together again.

When Mama hung up, we called Shyla back to tell her the good news. Dad put her on the speakerphone so we all could listen and talk.

"That's great, Dad," Shyla said, her voice thick with sleep. "Now life can go back to normal."

"You sound exhausted," Daddy said. "Are you getting enough rest?"

"You remember college," Shyla said. "There's never enough time for sleep." She yawned loudly. "Hey, Phoebe, don't forget to call me after the dance and give me all the details, okay?"

After we hung up, I went to my room and flopped onto my bed, feeling better than I had in months. The trial was over. I had survived the first weeks of freshman year. The dance was coming up, and Nick Harper liked me, sort of. Best of all, my mother was coming home, and when she did: *Ciao*, Beverly.

On Monday, Zane and I returned to school as minor celebrities due to the TV coverage about the trial and a long newspaper article that had been published the day before. Of course, Zane was already well known on campus, but until that day I was pretty much a freshman nobody. Now even sophomores and juniors were stopping to talk to me in the hall. I'd gone to school that morning expecting more gossip and name-calling, so to have so much positive attention was a pleasant surprise.

It also helped that there had been a huge controversy at the Second Baptist Church the night before. According to Bobby Hager, a sophomore football player who claimed to have witnessed the whole episode, a couple of the deacons went to the preacher after the Sunday-night service complaining that the choir director had been flirting with the new soprano, who lived with her husband, five kids, and a foul-tempered bulldog in a trailer house out on Buckner Road. The deacons said the church just couldn't abide such unseemly behavior in public, and something had to be done. Preacher Landrum backed up the choir director, who just happened to be his very own brother-in-law, and overnight the church had split into two camps—those who backed the preacher and his kin, and those who didn't. Second Baptist was the biggest church in Eden except for First Baptist, and it looked like there would soon be a Third Baptist. Now that the town had something new to gossip about, Judge Trask and his flag-burning communists were yesterday's news.

Even better, the moratorium against me had been lifted; Ash and Courtney saved me a seat at lunch. It was raining, so we were inside at long tables in the cafeteria.

As soon as I sat down, Ashley said, "You are not going to believe this. I am so bummed. My aunt Rita, up in Fort Worth, had her baby a whole month early, and now my mom says we have to go visit them this weekend."

"But you'll miss the dance!" Courtney said.

"Duh!" Ashley opened up her hamburger and scraped off all the chopped onions. "It's so unfair. I don't see why we have to go *this* weekend. The way I see it, that baby is going to be a baby for a good long while. What does it matter when we see him? Newborns all look the same anyway."

"Well, if you're not going to the dance, I'm not

going either," Courtney said. Then she glanced at me. "No offense, Phoebe. But you know how it is."

Even though I was irked, since I'd counted on them as my backup strategy, I knew what Courtney meant. Lauren and I had shared that same kind of loyalty. I picked at my Caesar salad. "Not a big deal."

"So, what are you wearing?" Ashley asked.

I described my new clothes and the earrings Beverly had picked out. Then Courtney asked about the assignment Madame Rochard had handed out last week, and we talked about homework and our upcoming tests until the bell rang, signaling the end of lunch.

Ashley grabbed her backpack. "See y'all in PE!"

Courtney went to the rest room. I ran up the stairs to my locker to dump a bunch of books and slid into my seat in world history five seconds before the tardy bell. Mr. Clifton roused himself from his postprandial stupor and fumbled with his lecture notes. "In the year 986," he began in a voice so boring I actually started looking forward to PE, "the Norse-men were the first to see North A-mer-i-ca, while seek-ing the set-tle-ment of Er-ic the Red."

I tried to concentrate, but I couldn't stop thinking about the fact that my mother was coming home. I was relieved that soon all would be well in the Land of Trask, that Beverly would no longer be trying to step in and take Mama's place, but now that my initial relief had worn off, I didn't feel the overwhelming elation I'd expected whenever I imagined her homecoming. Maybe I didn't miss my mother as much as I thought. Maybe what I missed was the *idea* of a mother who was always there to listen whenever I wanted to talk.

Mercifully, the bell finally rang, and I headed for science class, which turned out to be a bust because Nick was absent. Mrs. Grady assigned me to sit with a couple of other people as temporary lab partners. We took turns looking at a bunch of plant seeds through the microscope and drawing examples in our workbooks. I scribbled the names into my book, but I missed Nick. I hoped he hadn't gotten sick, or hurt in some freak accident that would prevent his coming to the dance.

In PE we were supposed to climb a rope as part of a physical-fitness test, but Ash and Courtney and I cracked up when Courtney kept sliding back down. The more the teacher told us to stop laughing, the funnier it got. Pretty soon everybody was laughing so hard nobody could climb the rope, and the teacher got mad and gave us all zeros for the day. As if we cared.

By the time I met Zane in the parking lot, my stomach felt sore from laughing so much. On the way home I told him everything that had happened that day, including my bad grade in PE. "So," I finished, "how was your day?"

He swung the Ford through the drive-in window at Gus's and ordered a couple of extra-large colas. "There's news in the Ginger department."

"Her dad is letting you date her for real?"

"Yeah." My brother tried to look like it was no big deal, but I could tell he was about to explode with happiness.

"That's great! So she'll be your date for the Halloween party after all."

"She has an early curfew, though. Mr. Threadgill says nothing good happens after ten p.m."

He paid for the sodas, and we drank them on the way home. I tackled my homework, and when it was done, I made some tea and took some hamburger patties out of the fridge for dinner, keeping one eye on the street. Even though things seemed to be settling down now that the trial was over, I still worried about Daddy until I saw his car coming up the drive at the end of the day.

He got home around six. We grilled the burgers and watched the Rangers game on TV. Zane left after the third inning and went over to the Threadgills'. Daddy fell asleep in his chair during the seventh-inning stretch. I took Lucky outside, then we went to my room, and I read for a while before finally falling asleep dreaming of Nick.

The rest of the week went by at a snail's pace, the way it always does when you're waiting for something important to happen. But at last Saturday came. Shyla called just as I was getting out of the shower. I wrapped my hair in a towel and sat on the edge of my bed while she peppered me with dos and don'ts, until I thought my head would bust open. I told her finally about Nick and about Caroline's backup theory, which Shyla said was a sound strategy. "She's right. You can't look like you're desperate for his attention. Let him make the first move."

"The problem is I have no backup!" I said. "The only two girls I really know are not going to the dance at all."

"Oh, I'll bet you know a lot more kids than you think," Shyla said. "You just can't be so shy about talking to them."

"But what will I say? I'm not good at small talk like you are."

"I don't know. Ask them who their favorite teacher is. What they thought of last night's football game."

"We lost," I said. "Mirabeau High beat us twenty-seven to zip."

"Oh. Might not want to bring that up, then," my sister said. "Listen, kiddo, I've got to run. I just wanted to wish you good luck tonight. Call me tomorrow, okay? Bye!"

I hung up and took my time getting dressed. When I was ready, Daddy took the pictures we'd promised Mama, and he drove me to the dance.

"I'll pick you up at ten thirty," he said as I opened the car door. "Have a great time, Feebs."

"It's *Phoebe,* Daddy." I got out of the car and hurried inside.

The cheerleaders had transformed the gym into a fake ranch, complete with bales of hay, cowboy boots, and a full-size papier-mâché longhorn steer. At one end of the gym they had set up tables holding cans of soda, boxes of pizza, and plates of cookies. In the middle of the table sat a huge cake with white icing and the word "HOWDY" spelled out in University of Texas orange. At the other end of the gym a spiky-haired deejay was spinning records.

"Here you go," one of the cheerleaders said, handing me a name tag printed with my name and, below that, in big letters, "HOWDY!"

I put the name tag on and looked around. So far the dance was shaping up pretty much the way Zane had described it, with the boys on one side of the room and the girls on the other. The doors leading to the girls' rest room were in constant motion. I looked for Nick, but he hadn't shown up yet. Katie and Gillian, Lauren's former friends, came in together. They waved to me, so I took a deep breath and went over to them.

"Hi," Katie said, eyeing my suede skirt and jacket. "Cute outfit."

"Thanks."

I just stood there, my brain suddenly stuck on

stupid. Gillian, who was wearing a pink dress, strappy sandals, and way too much glittery eye shadow, said, "The music sounds pretty good, don't you think?"

"Great," Katie and I said together.

Then Katie said, "Excuse me!" She grabbed Gillian's arm, nearly pulling her off her feet, and they headed for the rest room.

The deejay put on another song and said into the mic, "Okay, freshmen, let's get this party going. Everybody dance!"

A few couples moved onto the floor. The deejay turned the volume up, sending the sound bouncing off the walls.

"Phoebe?" said a voice in my ear. *Nick.*

I turned around, certain that he could actually see my heart beating through the fabric of my jacket. My mouth went dry as dirt. "Hi."

"Hi." He stuck his hands in his pockets, and we watched the dancers for a minute. Caroline's advice started running through my head. I looked around for somebody I could talk to, since it seemed like Nick wasn't going to ask me to dance. A line had formed outside the girls' rest room.

I said, "Excuse me," at the very same second Nick said, "Want to dance?"

"Okay."

He took my hand and led me onto the floor just as

the song ended. I let go of his hand, but he pulled me back. "Hold on."

Another tune started and we danced, concentrating on not mangling each other's feet. The song was an old one by the Eagles. Even though every time we discussed music, Ashley insisted they were way past hip, I totally loved their music, and I told Nick so. When it was over, Nick said, "Want a soda?"

And just like that we were a couple. We went to the refreshments table, and Nick got our sodas while I filled our plates. We found seats on a bale of hay near the chaperone's corner, and Mrs. Grady and Mr. Clifton glowered at us, like it was our fault they'd had to give up their Saturday night to make sure we didn't have too much fun.

Nick said, "I heard you and your friends got into trouble in PE the other day."

"Yeah." I almost cracked up again just telling him about it.

He told me he was thinking of going out for the basketball team next semester, and that his cousin in Houston had just turned sixteen and gotten a motorcycle. Then we ran out of topics, until I remembered something Shyla had once said, that the easiest way to make conversation with a boy is to ask him questions about himself. Then all you have to do is say "Really?" or "No way!" every few minutes, and he'll just keep going and going like that battery-powered rabbit in the TV commercials.

"Have you ever ridden a cycle before?" I asked, and the next time I looked at the clock, a whole hour had gone by. It was surreal, like I was standing outside watching myself laugh and talk and flirt with one of the cutest guys in the freshman class. Katie floated past on the arm of a lanky boy with stegosaurus hair who sat in the back row of Madame Rochard's class. Smiling like the cat that swallowed the canary, Katie waggled her fingers at me, and I waved back.

The deejay took a break, and the cheerleaders gave away some door prizes. Gillian won a pair of passes to the Eden movie theater, and a girl from Mr. Clifton's class won a coupon for free pizza. Katie's guy scored a certificate for a free CD from a music store downtown, and everybody got a coupon good for a dollar off our next purchase at Gus's.

The deejay came back and was three or four songs into the last set when Nick said, "Let's go outside."

We went out front, where a bunch of other kids were milling around talking, their voices muffled in the dark. A few couples had wandered out to the parking lot and were sitting on the curb, their backs to the building.

"You look really pretty," Nick said.

"Thanks. I got this outfit in Dallas. My neighbor

and I drove up there in her convertible. It's a great car." I knew I was babbling, but being there in the dark with such a completely awesome guy was making me nervous. He was standing so close I could feel his breath on my cheek.

Nick bent his head and his lips brushed mine, in a soft, warm kiss so quick that at first I thought I'd imagined it. I felt so strange, completely changed on the inside, as if I'd crossed a magical threshold into a different world. It was a moment I wanted to hold on to forever.

The outdoor floodlights blazed on, and Mrs. Cantrell's voice cut through the darkness, "Okay, people, back inside!"

We went back to the gym just as the deejay dimmed the lights and announced a slow song. Nick wound his arms around me as we moved to the music, and I wished this night could go on till the end of time. But the song ended, the lights came back up, and after one last fast song that got everybody moving Mrs. Cantrell wished us all a good night.

Nick and I joined the crowd heading for the exit. When we got outside, I spotted Daddy's car in the parking lot. "There's my ride."

"Okay. See you."

And before I could tell him how wonderful the whole night had been for me, and how I would never forget one single moment of it, Nick turned and walked away like nothing had happened.

I got into the car, wondering if Daddy could see that I was different, if he'd guess I'd had my first kiss. I was glad for the darkness that hid my face. Not that I was ashamed or anything. It's just that there are some things fathers are better off not knowing.

He pulled through the parking lot, and we started home. "Did you have a good time?" he asked.

"I had a great time."

Which was the biggest understatement of the century.

"So," Shyla began the next morning when I called to fill her in on the dance. "Did Nick kiss you?"

I'd stayed awake most of the night reliving every second of our time together, but I couldn't talk about it. Sharing it with anyone, even Shyla, would diminish it.

"I'll take that silence as a yes," Shyla said, laughing. "Did you meet any nice girls?"

"Not really. Mostly I hung out with Nick."

"Boys are great, but they can be fickle. Don't shut your girlfriends out of your life just to be with them."

"Yes, Mother."

"Okay, I get the message. No more advice. Tell me: Did they drag out that fake longhorn steer?"

"Yeah. Let's just say it has seen better days."

"No kidding. He was there at *my* Howdy Dance, and that's been a while. I bet they had door prizes and an orange-and-white cake, too, didn't they?"

"Why, Shyla Trask, you sound homesick."

A long sigh came over the phone. "Maybe I am. I'm tired of the grind, you know?"

"A barista tired of the grind. Very funny."

"Shut up. I'm being serious here."

"Sorry." I nudged Lucky aside and rolled over on my bed, sending a magazine and my algebra text sliding to the floor. "You could always take next semester off and come home. Mama would be thrilled."

"Yeah, but with all my AP credits, I'm close to finishing junior year. I should stick it out. I'm glad Mama's coming home, though. She sounds tired all the time. I'm worried about her."

I heard a series of clicks, and Shyla said, "Oops, there's my other line. Catch you later, kiddo. Glad you had a blast at the dance. Bye!"

I hung up and took Lucky outside. Zane was working on his car. The hood was up, tools were scattered everywhere, and the battery was sitting on the driveway. I pounded on the fender and he jumped.

"Jeez, Phoebe, don't *do* that!"

"Sorry. What are you doing?"

"Cleaning the battery cables. Toss me that wire brush."

I handed it to him. "Where's the judge?"

"Guess," my brother said grimly. He jerked his thumb, and then I saw Daddy and Beverly sitting on her front porch talking. "He's been over there for an hour."

"What are we going to do about it?"

"What *can* we do?" He attacked the corroded battery connections and wiped the gunk off with a rag. "If he's determined to make an ass of himself, we just have to put up with it till Mom gets back."

"Shyla's worried about Mama. Do you think she's sick?"

"Shyla?"

"*Mama,* you goof."

"Well, how was *I* supposed to know who you meant?" Zane tossed the rag onto the ground and lifted the battery into place. "Hand me that wrench."

He tightened the nuts and jiggled the battery. "That ought to do it."

Zane slammed the hood into place and gathered his tools.

"Zane," I persisted. "Do you think Mama's sick?"

The muscle in his jaw jumped the way it always did when he was mad. "Hard to tell, since in the last six months we've seen her for a grand total of fifteen minutes."

Beverly's laughter drifted across the yard. Daddy got up from her porch swing and came home. Lucky bounded over to him and dropped a Frisbee at Daddy's feet.

"Hey, boy." Daddy patted Lucky's head, tossed the Frisbee, and said to us, "How about lunch? I'm starved."

"I'm eating at Ginger's," Zane said. "Gotta hit the shower."

Daddy watched him jog up the driveway and into

the house. "What's bothering your brother?"

If I'd had the guts to confront Daddy right then, it would have saved a whole pack of problems, but without Zane to back me up I was too chicken to say anything. I shrugged. "Beats me."

Daddy said, "I guess that leaves you and me. Want to grab a burger at Gus's?"

A burger sounded good—wonderful, in fact—but I wasn't in the mood to make small talk with my father. "I have a ton of homework," I said. "Maybe we should make a sandwich or something."

"All right." Daddy whistled for Lucky. We went inside and made grilled cheese sandwiches. After we ate, I went to my room, got my homework out of the way, and spent the whole afternoon dreaming of Nick.

Monday morning everybody was still keyed up about the dance. As I was opening my locker, Ashley cornered me, demanding to know all the details about who had danced with whom, but since I'd spent the whole night totally absorbed in Nick, I couldn't tell her a whole lot. I described the deejay, the decorations, the door prizes, the cake that hardly anybody ate.

"That doesn't surprise me," Ashley said, stuffing books into her backpack. "Those cakes always look way better than they taste. My mom says the frosting is made mostly from shortening and powdered sugar.

Ugh." She made a face. "So, did you dance with anybody special?"

"Nick. We had a great time."

"You are so lucky!"

The bell rang. Ashley said, "See you at lunch!"

I headed for French class, counting the minutes till science lab and my first glimpse of Nick. Since he'd complimented me on my looks at the dance, I'd agonized over what to wear today, not wanting to disappoint him. I finally decided on the pink sweater from Beverly, with black jeans and an armload of chunky bracelets. I raided Mama's Bee Beautiful stash and picked out a new lipstick, a soft pink called Romantic Rose. After history, I raced to the rest room to brush my hair and reapply my lipstick. I popped a breath mint into my mouth and slid into my seat in the science lab just as the bell rang.

Which turned out to be a lot of trouble for nothing, as Nick was absent again, the third time he'd missed school on a Monday. Mrs. Grady shot me a dirty look as she sent me to sit with a couple of other students, like it was my fault my lab partner hadn't shown up.

That afternoon Zane dropped me at the bookshop downtown so I could replace the French/English dictionary I'd lost. I got a new one, plus a couple of paperbacks, then hung around downtown window-shopping, killing time until court let out and Daddy could take me home.

I ducked into a convenience store to buy a soda, and when I came out, Nick was heading into the drugstore on the corner. I jogged across the street and waited under the red awning until he came out.

"Nick! Hi!"

"Hi." He folded a flat white drugstore bag and shoved it into his jeans pocket. He kept his head down, but I could still see an ugly bruise at his temple.

"Are you okay? Everybody missed you at school today."

He started walking fast, and I hurried to keep up with him. "I'm fine, Phoebe," he muttered. "Just leave me alone, okay?"

"What happened to your face?"

He stopped. "Who are you, the freaking police?"

"No, but that bruise wasn't there on Saturday night. I would have noticed."

I touched his arm. "Tell me."

After a long silence he said, "It's my dad. Most of the time he's okay, you know? He takes Jacob fishing and shows up at my football games like he's the all-American dad. But when he drinks, he turns into a monster, yelling at us, swearing at Mom and hitting her. I try to keep him away from her when he gets like that, but he's a lot bigger than me."

"That's horrible. Can't he get help, like at AA or something?"

"He won't go to the meetings. He promises he will, but when the time comes, he says nothing is wrong with him and she should get off his back about it." He raked the hair out of his eyes. "Weekends are the worst."

"That's why you're absent on Mondays."

"Yeah. After his binges Mom is usually in pretty bad shape. She won't let me call the cops. I don't know what to do."

"We should talk to my dad. He knows the law. He can help."

"No! If Pop finds out I've told *anybody* our business, he'll make it worse for all of us. You can't say anything, Phoebe. Promise me you won't."

"I promise. But think about talking to my dad. He's good at keeping secrets. Maybe he can figure out some way to help without your dad finding out."

"Listen, I gotta go."

"Okay. See you tomorrow, I guess."

"Yeah." He managed a weak grin. "I had a great time Saturday night. Before I got home, I mean."

"Me too."

He headed down the street, past my dentist's office and a jewelry store. At the corner he turned back to me. "You want to hang out at the Halloween carnival this year?"

"Sure."

I watched him until he disappeared onto

Thornton Avenue, then I crossed the street and walked to the courthouse to meet Daddy, torn between wanting to keep my promise to Nick and feeling that I should find some way to help him.

On the way home my father seemed too preoccupied to ask a million questions about my day, the way he usually did. Most of the time I thought it was a huge pain to have to fill him in on everything, until he didn't ask and I realized how much I looked forward to telling him what all was going on in my life. Well, most of it, anyway.

"Tough day, Daddy?" I asked as we waited for the traffic light to change.

"No more than usual. Just a couple of annoying phone calls."

"Hang-ups, like before?"

"No. This time the caller had plenty to say." He patted my knee. "Don't worry about it. A judge can't please all the people all the time. Criticism comes with the job."

He seemed in control of the situation, so I didn't let it worry me too much. I thought about school, homework, and my plans for taking in the Halloween carnival with Nick. Zane had promised to drop me at the carnival on his way to pick up Ginger, and Daddy would drive me home after.

The next few weeks went by in a blur of classes, pep rallies, and homework projects. When carnival night came, Zane grabbed his keys and the box containing his rented costume, and we headed for the school. He didn't say much on the way there, but I could tell he was excited to be spending the evening with Ginger, even though they'd have to leave the party early to make it back to Eden by her curfew. Zane pulled into the driveway and stopped. "Here you go, kiddo. Have fun, but don't do anything dumb, okay?"

"Same to you." I got out of the car and closed the door. Zane shot me a grin and peeled onto the highway.

It was warmer than normal for the end of October, and Mrs. Cantrell had decided to move the carnival outside. Tables laden with food and beverages were set up on a grassy field adjacent to the football stadium. The hay bales from the Howdy Dance were decorated with plastic jack-o'-lanterns and a grinning skeleton that danced when you walked by him.

A bonfire was blazing, and the band was tuning up. Ash and Courtney were sitting on a hay bale with Katie, Gillian, and a couple of other girls I didn't know, drinking hot cider from Styrofoam cups. They waved me over. Ashley scooted over to make room for me. "Hey, Phoebe. Where's Nick?"

"He's coming later."

"I'm so jealous," Courtney said. "You're the first girl in our class to have a boyfriend."

I wasn't sure how to describe my relationship with Nick. Since we lived so far apart, I saw him mostly at school, and sometimes he put up an invisible wall between us that left me feeling confused. Still, it felt great to be considered half of a couple. I looked out across the field. People were roasting marshmallows over the bonfire, sending the smell of burned sugar into the air. "I'm starving," I said. "What's to eat?'

"The usual," Courtney said. "Pizza and ice cream."

"But," Ashley said with a grin, "there is no Howdy cake."

"There is, however, a Happy Halloween cake," Katie said. "It's probably the same one, recycled."

A boy from French class sidled over to us and said, "Hey, Courtney."

"Hi, Dexter."

"Um. You want to hang out?"

"Sure. Okay." She handed Ashley her cup. "See you later."

They moved off into the dark. Ashley said, "*Dexter?* What parents in their right mind would name a kid Dexter?"

"You're just jealous," Katie teased. "I think he's adorable, in a geeky kind of way. Come on. Let's eat."

"I'm going to listen to the band," Gillian said. "Catch you later."

Ashley, Katie, and I went to the tables and got

some pizza. I had just taken a huge bite when Nick walked up behind me and said, "There you are."

"Hi, Nick!" Katie and Ashley said together.

Then Ashley said, with a mischievous grin, "We're so relieved you're finally here. Phoebe was about to expire waiting for you to show up. If you hadn't turned up when you did, we'd have had to give her CPR."

"Very funny, Ashley." I offered Nick a bite of pizza.

"I'm not hungry," he said. "Let's go listen to the band."

Nick and I walked across the field and sat on the grass, our shoulders touching, close enough to the fire to feel its heat but far enough away that we were deep in the shadows. A few kids milled nearby, joking with the band.

"Are you okay?" I asked quietly. "Is your dad—"

"Sober when I left. But I heard him tell Mom he was going out with a couple of friends, so who knows how long that will last."

"I still wish you'd let me tell my dad what's going on. I know he'd want to help."

"Telling the judge would be a big mistake. Pop has a major problem with authority figures."

"But that's not rational."

"Drunks aren't exactly known for being rational," Nick said. "Besides, what could your dad do if Mom won't press charges? Back in Houston our neighbors called the cops a couple of times when they heard Mom and Pop fighting, but Mom told everybody to mind their own business. She thinks one day Pop will just magically decide to stop drinking and everything will be perfect." He shook his head. "I love her a lot, you know? But sometimes I hate her because she's living in a dreamworld."

We listened to the music. When the band finished the first set, Nick stood. "I have to go. Pop promised to take Jacob trick-or-treating, then backed out when his friends called. I told Jacob I'd take him, and it's getting pretty late for him."

"I could come with you."

"Really?" His smile nearly broke my heart. "That would be so great, Phoebe. I'll grab Jacob, and we'll meet you in front of the gym. Ten minutes, okay?"

We hurried back across the grass and into the glow of floodlights outside the gym. A group of kids had gathered near the entrance, talking and laughing. Nick loped across the street and disappeared into the dark. I checked my watch. It was only a few minutes past nine. I figured we'd take Jacob on his extortion mission and I'd be back at school in plenty of time for Dad to pick me up at ten thirty.

A car rounded the corner and screeched to a stop at the curb not ten feet away. I looked up as Beverly jumped out of the car and ran through the crowd, calling my name. I knew then that something was terribly wrong. In the few seconds it took her to reach me, my first thought was that Zane had wrecked his car or been hit by some crazy person out drinking and driving.

"Beverly?" I pressed my hand to my chest to keep my heart from jumping out. "What's wrong?"

I was already starting to cry when she put her arms around me and said, "Phoebe, honey, it's your dad."

One summer Daddy and Mama decided that their kids should see the U.S. capital, and we headed for Washington, D.C. After we'd toured the important buildings and the monuments to Washington, Lincoln, and Jefferson, we drove all the way to Connecticut to see one of Daddy's old friends from his law school days. Mr. Sawyer ("Sawyer the lawyer," Shyla called him) lived in a white house with a rolling green lawn surrounded by a crumbling stone wall that looked as if it had been there since God was a baby. Here and there you could see gaps in the wall where one of the gray, moss-furred stones had fallen out. When I asked Daddy why the whole thing didn't collapse, he said that when one stone fell, the others shifted to keep the rest in place.

As Beverly and I raced toward the hospital, the neon signs and orange Halloween lights in the store windows passing in a blur, I thought back to the year that Shyla had first gone off to the university and we'd had to adjust to an empty place at the dinner table.

Shift. When Mama left, we shifted again, trying to fill the space her going had made in our lives. Now Zane and I were leaning on our father, the only constant we had left. If we lost him, the Trask family, what was left of it, would crumble and fall.

"What happened?" I asked as we neared the hospital and Beverly slowed to turn into the parking lot.

"He was working late, and when he went out to his car, a gang of thugs jumped him. They beat him pretty bad, but he was able to call me. I called the paramedics and the police." She took a ticket from the automatic gate and tucked it into her purse.

"But he'll be okay, right?"

"I hope so, honey."

As soon as Beverly had parked, I was out of the car and racing for the door to the emergency room. She came in right behind me and told the nurse at the desk that we were there to see Judge Trask, and we took the elevator to the second floor. The waiting room was not much bigger than my room at home. It had a ratty sofa, a coffee table littered with old magazines, and a couple of orange plastic chairs. In the corner sat a vending machine and a coffeemaker. The TV bolted to the wall was tuned to a football game, the sound turned all the way down. I watched the fans silently cheering their team.

A doctor strode down the hall toward us, his white

coat flapping loose behind him. When he saw Beverly, he said, "Mrs. Trask?"

"No, I'm a family friend. This is Judge Trask's daughter."

The doctor barely nodded to me.

"Is my dad okay?" My voice sounded high and strange in my ears.

"He has a concussion, a broken collarbone, some lacerations on his face and hands, a couple of bruised ribs. We're waiting on the X-rays to check for internal injuries, but I'm hopeful that the head wound and the broken collarbone are the worst of it."

"Can I see him?"

"He's fairly medicated. He may not be able to talk much, but you can see him."

The doctor led us down the hall to a dimly lit room. We went in, and the sight of my father swathed in white and attached to a bunch of machines just about did me in. Tears streamed down my face as Beverly and I approached the bed.

"Daddy?" I bent over him and spoke above the *beep-beep-beep* of the machines.

"Feebs." His eyes opened. "Don't cry."

"Who did this, Daddy?"

His head moved back and forth on the stark white pillow. "Too dark. Couldn't see."

"Sum-nuh," Beverly said softly. "We should phone

your wife and your other children. Do you have their numbers somewhere?"

"I have them," I said, reaching into my purse for my cell phone.

"No," Daddy said in a surprisingly strong voice. "Don't call Beth."

"But Mama has to know!" I said. "She'll want to come home."

Daddy sat up in bed, and the doctor hurried over. "Judge Trask, lie still. You'll pull your IVs out."

"I don't want my wife to know about this!" Daddy said. "Not yet."

"All right," the doctor said. "Calm down and we'll talk about it later."

He turned to Beverly and me. "He should rest. You can wait outside if you want."

We went back out to the waiting room, and I punched in Zane's cell number, but when he answered, I started bawling so hard I couldn't talk. Beverly took the phone and explained what had happened. I heard her tell him to drive carefully, and she hung up.

"He's on his way," she said. "Shall I call Shyla for you?"

"Okay." As much as I hated the way Beverly had intruded into our lives, I will admit that right then it felt good to have an adult in charge.

I listened as Beverly called the coffeehouse and asked for Shyla. A couple of minutes later she hung up and said, "Shyla's leaving Austin right now. She'll be here before morning."

Beneath the stark hospital lights Beverly looked pale and drawn. She put her arm around me, and despite myself, I leaned into her soft, warm shoulder.

"Now," she said, "what should we do about calling your mother?"

Even though I wanted my mother more than anything, I said, "Daddy will be really mad if we go behind his back. I guess we should wait, like he said."

"I suppose you're right. He doesn't seem to be in any immediate danger." She peered into the glass coffeepot. "I could use some coffee, but not this sludge. I think I'll go down to the cafeteria. Want to come?"

"I'd rather wait here for Zane."

"All right. I won't be long."

She got on the elevator. The door whooshed shut. I sat down on the threadbare sofa and thumbed through a magazine, but the words danced on the page. My emotions were a mishmash of fear, relief, and fury at whoever had hurt my dad.

A grizzled old guy shuffled into the waiting room and sat down across from me. He took off his baseball cap, picked up the TV remote, and flipped through the channels, watching the montage of silent images flash past. Finally he shrugged, muttered, "Nothing to watch," and fell asleep sitting upright in the chair.

A nurse walked by, flipped the channel back to the

football game, checked the score, and left. A few minutes later the elevator doors opened, and Nick got off. I jumped up. "Oh, my gosh! I'm sorry! I was supposed to go trick-or-treating with you."

"That's not important right now. Are you okay? How's your dad?"

That was just like Nick to focus on what was most important. My eyes welled up. "He looks awful! Who would *do* something like this?"

"It's pretty cowardly." Nick dropped onto the sofa, pulling me down beside him. "Are you here by yourself?"

I explained that Beverly had picked me up at school and now we were waiting for Zane and Shyla. "But how did you know?"

"It was all over the local news when I got Jacob home from trick-or-treating. Will Harte gave me a ride over here."

"I'm glad you came."

He laced his fingers through mine. "I had to know that you were okay."

We watched the silent football game for a few minutes. People came and went on the elevator. A couple of nurses strolled by. A phone rang. Beverly came back from the cafeteria with her coffee and a soft drink with crushed ice for me. I introduced her to Nick, and she said, "I'm happy to meet a friend of Phoebe's. If I'd known you were here, I'd have brought you something. But there's soda in the machine over there if you're thirsty."

"That's okay." Nick stood. "I have to go. Mom will worry if I'm out too late."

"How will you get home?" I asked.

"It's not that far. I can walk."

"Are you sure?" Beverly asked.

"Don't worry about me. I'm used to looking out for myself."

I walked with him to the elevator. "Thanks for coming. I'm sorry about trick-or-treating."

"It's no big deal. There's always next year, right?"

In spite of the situation with Daddy, I felt a thrill just knowing that Nick was thinking that far ahead into our relationship.

"Yeah. We'll make up for it next year."

He pushed the button to summon the elevator. When the door slid open, he said, "See you."

Then he was gone.

Beverly curled up on the sofa, one leg tucked under her, and sipped her coffee. "Nick seems very nice, Phoebe, and more mature than most boys his age."

I thought about everything Nick had to deal with at home. Trying to keep your father from killing your mother would make a person grow up in a hurry. I wanted so badly to help him and hated that I was sworn to silence. I sipped my soft drink.

The elevator dinged, the doors opened yet again,

and Zane and Ginger rushed into the waiting room, still dressed in the pirate costumes they'd worn to the party. "Where's Dad?" Zane asked.

I pointed down the hall. "He's asleep. Shyla's coming home, but he won't let me call Mama."

"That's crazy." Zane looked pointedly at Beverly, who said, "I agree with you, Zane, but your father was quite insistent he doesn't want your mother contacted just yet."

"I want to see him."

We started down the dim, hushed hallway. "He looks pretty bad," I warned.

Beverly opened the door to Dad's room, and we tiptoed in. Zane gasped when he saw Daddy lying beneath the tightly drawn sheets. Bathed in the glow of the beeping monitors, Daddy's bruised and bandaged face was a sickly shade of green.

"Man," Zane whispered. "Somebody really did a number on him." He turned to Beverly. "Do the cops know who did it?"

"I don't think they know anything yet, but they'll find out, Zane. And whoever did this will pay."

"Damn right they will." Zane gripped Daddy's bed frame so hard his knuckles turned white.

"Zane?" Ginger whispered. "I hate to bring this up, since we just got here, but it's getting really late. If I miss my curfew—"

"I know."

"We should all go home," Beverly whispered. "Your daddy will sleep till morning anyway, and we're exhausted."

We went out to the parking lot. Zane left to take Ginger home, and I got into Beverly's car. When we pulled into the driveway ten minutes later, the house was dark. Beverly let the car idle in the driveway. "Want me to come inside with you, sugar?"

Knowing that whoever had attacked Daddy was still out there made me nervous, but I didn't want to show it. "That's okay. Zane will be home in a few minutes."

"If you need anything, just holler."

"I will." I got out and shut the car door. "Thanks for everything."

She waited while I unlocked the door and switched on some lights. Lucky came charging out and jumped up, whining and wagging his tail. I poured him some food and drank a glass of milk while he ate.

Then Zane came in and tossed his keys onto the kitchen counter. "That was close! Mr. T. was practically standing in the driveway with his stopwatch when we pulled in."

"I hope Ginger told him you had an emergency."

"Yeah. He'd already heard it on the news. He says the cops are talking to three guys who were hanging around the bars downtown. Apparently, one of them was bragging that they'd gotten even with the judge."

Three guys in a bar. My stomach dipped. Nick's dad and his friends had been out tonight. And hadn't Nick said his father had a problem with authority figures?

"What?" Zane said.

"Nothing. You want some milk?"

"Nah, I just want to get out of this ridiculous costume."

He started up the stairs. "Are you going to bed?"

"I can't sleep. I'll wait for Shyla."

Zane went upstairs, and I took Lucky outside. While he sniffed around, I watched clouds sliding across the hunter's moon and wondered who had hurt my dad. Even though, with some people still fuming about the trial, there were plenty of candidates in Eden, I couldn't shake the suspicion that Nick's father was involved, which would be just one more disaster in my rapidly deteriorating life.

Lucky pawed the door, and we went back inside. I grabbed a pink-and-white afghan Mama had knit when I was a baby, and curled up on the couch with Lucky. I flipped through the sports channels and the movie channels, then checked out the Beauty Channel, but nothing captured my interest. I fell asleep listening for Shyla's car.

When I woke up, sunlight was streaming through the window, and she was in the kitchen making breakfast. Lucky was sitting beside the fridge, hoping for a handout.

"Hey," she said softly when I sat up. "Are you okay, kiddo?"

"I guess so. What time did you get here?"

"Around one o'clock. You were sleeping so soundly I didn't want to wake you."

I yawned. "You've been up all night?"

"Pretty much. I called the hospital to check on Dad as soon as I got in, and then I flaked out for a couple of hours. I'm okay."

"What did they say?"

"Still out like a light, which is probably the best thing right now."

She took eggs and butter out of the fridge. "Are you hungry?"

"Starved."

"Go see if Zane wants to eat. I'm only cooking once."

"I definitely want to eat," Zane said from the doorway. He waved to Shyla. "Hey, sis."

"Hey, Zaney-brainy."

"Don't call me that. I hate it. Besides, you're the brainy one around here." Zane opened the fridge and got the OJ carton.

"Actually, I'm beginning to question my own intelligence." Shyla broke a bunch of eggs into the skillet and loaded bread into the toaster. "A person would have to be crazy to take a full class load, plus a job at Jazz-n-Java, plus start an internship in the senator's office."

"Congratulations!" Zane said, pouring three glasses of orange juice. "Dad says those internships are hard to come by."

"I was lucky. Dad about busted his buttons when I told him I got it."

We were quiet then, thinking about our father. Shyla spooned the scrambled eggs into a serving bowl and got out a platter for the toast. We sat down just as Beverly appeared with a thermos of coffee and a basket of baked goods.

"I brought you something to eat," she said when Shyla opened the door for her. "I thought you'd be too worn out to cook."

"That's nice of you," Shyla said, "but we're fine. I've just made toast and eggs."

"Oh. Well, why don't you take these anyway. The pastries will keep for a while."

I was positive that Beverly was waiting for Shyla to ask her to come in and eat with us, but finally Beverly said, "I won't keep you. I'm sure you're anxious to get to the hospital and see your father."

"Yes," Shyla said, taking the basket from Beverly. "Thanks for thinking of us."

Shyla closed the door and set the basket on the counter. We finished our breakfast, got dressed, and drove to the hospital.

Daddy wasn't in his room when we got there; the nurse said they had taken him to get more X-rays. We sat around the waiting room for more than an hour before we saw an orderly pushing Daddy's wheelchair down the hallway.

Shyla ran down the hall and tried to hug him, but the tubes and the tall metal pole the orderly was pushing along beside him got in the way.

"Careful," the orderly said. He was a huge guy with a shaved head, a neat brown beard, and a plastic name tag that said MIKE.

"Shyla!" Daddy said. "You didn't have to drive all this way."

Shyla planted a kiss on his head. "I had to see for myself that you were okay."

"I'm going to be fine." Daddy still looked awful, but he seemed stronger. And there was good news from the X-rays: no more broken bones. "They're letting me out of here tomorrow," he said after Mike had settled him into his bed.

"But the doctor says you're to stay in bed for the next ten days," Mike reminded him. "You lost quite a bit of blood. Your collarbone needs time to heal, and you don't want to take a chance of fracturing those ribs."

Daddy waved his hand the way he did in court when he got impatient with a lawyer. "I have too much to do to lie about doing nothing."

"Orders are orders, that's all I'm saying." Mike parked the wheelchair in the corner and left, his sneakers squeaking on the tile floor.

"Well, Dad, this is one time you're going to have to let someone else be in charge," Shyla said. "Now, what's this nonsense about your not wanting Mama to know what happened? If she were sick or hurt, wouldn't you want to know?"

"Of course. But this is different."

"No, it isn't. You know I'm right."

"Yeah," Zane said. "What are we supposed to tell Mama when she calls?"

"I suppose I'll have to tell her something," Daddy admitted. "But I do *not* want her coming home on my account. February is not that far off, and I want her to come home when she's ready, not out of a sense of obligation."

But wasn't that what families were all about, bound by love and duty to take care of one another? Or were you supposed to be selfless enough just to step out of the picture so nothing came between a person and their dreams?

The door opened, and Beverly came in with a huge basket of yellow and white flowers.

"Good mornin', Sum-nuh!" she caroled. "I brought you something to liven up this joint."

"Thanks," Daddy said. "They're beautiful, but I'll be out of here tomorrow. They're releasing me on my own recognizance."

"That's wonderful news!" She dropped her sunglasses into her bag, set the basket on the windowsill, and beamed at all of us. "Good morning, Trasks!"

"Hi," we said.

Beverly set her purse down like she intended to stay awhile. "Now, Sum-nuh," she began. "I saw your doctor in the hallway just now, and he tells me you're to be on bed rest for the next several days."

"Yes," Daddy said. "I'm hiring a private-duty nurse to give me a hand while Phoebe and Zane are at school."

"Well, that's just ridiculous. Why waste good money when I'm sitting right next door with hardly anything to do?"

"What about your book?" I asked. "You *said* you came to Eden to get your work done."

"And I did!" Beverly crowed. "I finished it last week and shipped the whole shebang off to my editor. The ball is in his court now, and in the meantime I am completely at loose ends." She patted Daddy's covers. "I'll be happy to look after you till you're on your feet again."

"Phoebe and I can manage," Zane said. "We'll be okay."

Daddy said, "What about your swim meet, Zane? Don't you have an important one next week?"

"Yeah, but—"

"No buts," Dad said firmly. "I won't have you missing it on my account. And Phoebe should concentrate on her homework, not on fetching and carrying for me."

"But I don't mind, Daddy!"

"I know. But I've got this all worked out so I won't inconvenience anyone, and that's the end of it."

Just then the door opened, and the nurse came in wheeling a metal cart. "Okay, everybody out while I get this man's dressings changed. You can come back in half an hour."

Shyla bent over Daddy's bed. "I hate to leave, but I've got an exam tomorrow and a major paper due next week. Professor Gray will probably give me an extension on the paper, but if I miss Hartwell's exam . . ."

"Go," Daddy said. "I'm glad you came all this way to check on your old man, but I'm fine."

"I'll come back next weekend," Shyla said tearfully. "I love you, Daddy."

"Love you too. Drive carefully. Stop and rest when you get tired." He motioned to me and Zane. "I want the two of you to go on to school too. There's nothing you can do here, and I'll be sleeping most of the day anyhow. Those pain pills knock me for a loop."

"He's right," the nurse said. "Another hour and he'll be sleeping like a baby."

We said our good-byes and went home. I wished that Shyla could have stuck around, especially since she had driven practically half the night to get home, but she ran inside, grabbed her stuff, and headed for Austin. Zane and I went to school.

We pulled into the parking lot about twenty minutes before the end of second period. Too wrung out for conversation, we sat in the car waiting for the bell to ring, watching a couple of squirrels playing chase in the oak trees. When the bell sounded, Zane sighed and said, "Here we go."

Inside the building people parted for us like we were royalty. Everybody had heard about the attack on Judge Trask, and the questions flew fast and furious. Did we know who did it? Had we talked to the police? Was it true that our dad was in a coma? Someone had heard he'd been shot. Somebody else had heard he'd died. By lunchtime I was so sick of the questions I wanted to wear a sign around my neck warning people away.

Thankfully, Ashley and Courtney didn't ask a bunch of questions. Ash just asked if I was okay, and when I said I was, Courtney changed the subject to something with more immediate relevance: Namely, had I finished the homework assignment for Mr. Clifton's class, and could she borrow it?

I opened my notebook and slid it across the table. "Don't get grease all over it."

"I won't." Courtney wiped her fingers on her napkin, took out her pen, and scribbled on her paper. "Thanks. I owe you one."

Just as I was putting my paper away, I looked up and saw Nick coming into the cafeteria. I smiled and waved to him, but he looked right past me. That hurt. And I was embarrassed that Ash and Courtney saw how he had snubbed me.

"What's with him?" Courtney asked.

"Who knows?" I picked up my tray. "I gotta go."

"Hey," Ashley said. "Courtney's mom is driving us to the mall on Saturday. You want to come?"

It was the first time I'd been invited, and I really wanted to go. "Maybe. It depends on how my dad is doing."

"I forgot. Stupid me." Ashley picked up her tray. "I hope he's okay, Phoebe."

"Thanks. I'll let you know about Saturday."

I put my tray away and went to the rest room, wondering what I'd done to make Nick mad at me. He'd said he understood why I didn't go trick-or-treating with him and Jacob, but obviously something had happened. I couldn't wait to get to science class so that I could talk to him and get to the bottom of his weird behavior.

Mr. Clifton's class seemed longer and more boring than ever. I answered a question about the Roman Empire and handed in my homework without really thinking about it. When the bell rang, I hurried to science class, where Mrs. Grady spent half the period lecturing before finally releasing us for our lab work. I got our equipment and read through the lab manual, waiting for Nick to leave his chair at the back of the room and take his seat on the stool next to mine. Finally he did.

"Hi," I said.

He just stared at me.

"What's wrong? Why are you avoiding me?"

"Did you send the police to my house?"

"The police? No!" I said so loudly that Mrs. Grady looked up and frowned at us. "No," I said more softly. "Why would I?"

He shoved his hair out of his eyes. "Somebody thinks Pop is the one who beat up your dad."

"I heard they were questioning some men who were at a bar downtown, and I admit, the thought crossed my mind, but Nick, I didn't say *anything*. I swear."

"Just so you know," he said coldly, "Pop couldn't have been the one who did it, because he was too busy beating up on my mom at the time."

"I'm sorry. Is she hurt?"

"No broken bones. This time."

Mrs. Grady came by and rested her hand my shoulder. "How's the experiment coming, Phoebe?"

"We're just getting started."

"So I see." She snapped her fingers. "Time is running out. You'd better get a move on."

Nick opened his lab manual, and we hurried through the experiment. When the bell rang, instead of heading for his math class, he followed me to the gym. He grabbed my hand and pulled me to the side of the building, which was shaded by tall hedges. The marching band was practicing for Friday's game; music drifted across the field.

"I'm sorry," he said.

And before I could tell him it was okay, that I understood, he kissed me. It wasn't short and sweet like the first one. It was long and mixed with sadness. I pulled away, feeling shaken and exhilarated all at the same time.

"I have to go." My voice cracked. "I'll be late."

"Me too."

I don't remember anything else about that day. I must have gone to the hospital after school to see Daddy. I suppose that Zane and I stopped at Gus's for a burger when we got hungry. But my mind was so taken with Nick and his problem, Nick and the way he had kissed me, that everything else was a blur.

On Friday, when Zane and I got home from school, Daddy was already home, propped up in the living room on a rented hospital bed so he wouldn't have to climb the stairs to his room. The nurse he'd hired bustled around him straightening pillows, filling his water glass, and generally trying to convince him she was worth the money he was paying her.

When Daddy introduced us, she said, "I made a roast beef sandwich for his supper. It's in the fridge. I don't cook for the whole family, and I don't do laundry."

"We'll be fine, Mrs. Vance," Daddy said. "Thank you for coming."

"Well." She surveyed the room and straightened a stack of magazines on the coffee table. "All right, then. Don't forget your medications, Judge. They're right there on the table by your water glass."

"I'll remember."

"And use that walker when you have to go to the bathroom. One fall and those ribs of yours will shatter like glass. We wouldn't want that, would we?"

"No, ma'am." Behind her back Daddy winked at me.

Mrs. Vance pointed her finger at Zane and me. "Don't you kids make a lot of noise. Your father has been through an ordeal. He needs peace and quiet."

She picked up her yellow flowered tote bag and let herself out.

"Man, she's something else," Zane said. "Where did you find her, Dad?"

"The hospital recommended her," Daddy said. "Hey, Feebs, would you mind bringing that stack of papers from my desk?"

"You're supposed to rest."

"I *am* resting! It won't hurt me to read for a while."

Zane rummaged around in the kitchen and came out with a bag of chips and a can of soda. "Dad? I'm heading out to practice and then to Ginger's, okay?"

"Home by eleven," Daddy said.

I brought Daddy his papers. While he read, I

spread out my homework at the dining-room table. Later we ate our sandwiches in the living room.

"How are things at school?" Daddy asked.

"A couple of girls invited me to go to the mall with them tomorrow. Is it okay?"

"I don't see why not."

After calling Courtney, I switched on the lights and tried to watch TV, but there was nothing on but football and mindless sitcoms with sound tracks to tell you when to laugh. I was too preoccupied with everything else going on in my life to concentrate on anything anyway.

Daddy's papers rustled. "Phoebe?"

"Yeah, Daddy, do you need something?"

"What's the matter, sunshine? I've been talking to you for the last ten minutes."

"Sorry. I had a long day at school."

"Trouble with math again?"

"No more than usual."

"You want to talk about it?"

I wrapped Mama's old afghan around my shoulders. "Suppose somebody you cared about was in a bad situation and they made you promise not to tell."

"If you promised, then I'd say you have to keep your word. Unless you could convince this person to release you from your obligation. Of course, if he or she were involved in something illegal, then you'd have to tell, to avoid becoming a part of the crime."

Daddy peered at me over the top of his reading glasses. "Is someone you know in trouble?"

Just then Mama called, and she and Daddy talked for a long time. I thumbed through a magazine, listening to Daddy's side of the conversation. Now that we knew for sure when my mother was coming home, it seemed that something had loosened inside them both, and they were talking more easily, like in the old days. I thought about telling Daddy as much of Nick's situation as I could without actually giving anything away, but by the time they hung up, Daddy was worn out and I had lost my nerve.

The next morning, Saturday, Mrs. Vance didn't show up, so Zane and I made oatmeal and bacon for breakfast. While Zane helped Daddy to the bathroom, I made the bed, filled the water pitcher, and neatened up Daddy's stack of mail and papers.

Zane left for his swim meet. I was waiting for Ash and Courtney to pick me up for our trip to the mall when Beverly arrived with coffee and croissants. As if without her we'd starve to death.

"We've already eaten," I said.

"But those smell so good I might have to try one anyway," Daddy said from his bed. "Come on in, Bev, and have a seat."

"You're looking ever so much better," Beverly said, settling onto the sofa. "And I see you're starting to think about work already."

"Three days down, seven to go," he said like a kid counting down to Christmas. "I can't wait to get back to the courthouse."

Beverly put a croissant on a napkin and passed it to Daddy. "Do the police have any leads on who did this?"

"The chief called yesterday. He's questioning some people, looking into their alibis. Nothing solid yet."

The phone rang and Daddy picked it up. He listened for a minute and said, "Well, I'm sorry too. This puts me in a tough situation. It'll be difficult to find someone else on a weekend."

He listened some more. "In that case, perhaps it would be for the best."

He hung up. "Mrs. Vance quit. She's had second thoughts about taking care of me. She doesn't feel safe looking after someone so controversial."

"That's the silliest thing I've ever heard," Beverly said. "Who on earth would want to harm her?"

For once I agreed with Beverly. "That's okay, Dad," I said. "We don't need her. We can manage until Monday."

I picked up the phone. "I'll call Courtney and tell her I can't go to the mall today."

Beverly said, "Phoebe Trask, you'll do no such thing! I'll be happy to stay right here and look after your daddy."

Yes, I thought. *I just bet you would.*

"I don't mind. I can go to the mall anytime."

But just then Courtney's mom pulled into the driveway and honked the horn. Beverly said, "You go on, now. Have a good time, and don't worry about your daddy. I'll spoil him rotten."

That was only the beginning. For the next week Beverly practically lived at our house. She cooked elaborate meals, including dessert, every night. She took Daddy to the hospital for his follow-up appointment and refilled his prescriptions at the drugstore. She sat in on his talk with the police chief, organized our mail, and answered the phone. At night she watched TV with us or listened to opera records with Daddy until bedtime. In other words, she acted like a wife, like a mother, like someone who belonged in our family.

All that togetherness about drove Zane and me crazy, but Daddy soaked up the attention the way pancakes soak up syrup. And I have to admit, having Beverly there made life run smoother. Instead of rushing home right after school, Zane and I could act like normal teenagers, hanging out at Gus's, going to the movies and the football game.

Still, I couldn't wait for February, when Mama would come home.

Mama likes to say that every cloud has a silver lining, and maybe it's true. One year I missed Lauren's birthday party because Daddy's aunt Reba was visiting, and as a result I was the only one of Lauren's friends who avoided chicken pox. More recently, Zane's run-in with the law had sure improved his relationship with Daddy, which made things around the house a lot less tense.

The week before Thanksgiving break the huge black cloud that had hovered over Nick's family finally gave up its silver lining, and it happened because of the attack on my father. Daddy had been back at work for a few days, as good as new except for some sore ribs and a pale, moon-shaped scar just above his eyebrow. He was so focused on the next case coming up for trial that he didn't spend too much time worrying about his attackers. But the police chief and the county sheriff were like men possessed. It was a point of pride for them to solve the case. They had taken statements from half the population of

Eden, and every day one of them went on the local news to reassure the town that they were close to making an arrest.

Eventually the investigation focused on the three men who had been seen outside the bar, bragging about how Daddy had gotten what he deserved, and as I had feared, one of those three was Nick's dad, Frank Harper. According to Nick, the police were just about to arrest Mr. Harper and charge him with assault and battery, public drunkenness, and who knows what all, when Mrs. Harper showed up at the police station and confirmed for the cops what Nick had told me earlier—that her husband could not have been the one who beat up the judge. He was at home that night beating the tar out of her. She still had plenty of bruises to prove it.

"Man, I have never seen Pop as mad as he was when Mom told the cops what had been going on at the house," Nick said.

We were sitting outside in the quad, killing time before the last pep rally of football season. The sun was out, but a sharp wind bit into my shoulders as we huddled on one of the benches. I blew on my hands to warm them and turned my face to the sun.

"So, what happens now?" I asked.

"Mom made Pop move out until he completes a program at AA and takes anger management classes."

"That's good, don't you think?"

"Maybe. He's promised to change a bunch of times and never followed through."

"But your mom never made him leave the house before, right? That should get his attention."

"Yeah." Nick squeezed my hand. "I'm glad Pop wasn't involved in what happened to your dad. I wouldn't want you to be mad at me."

One of the coaches opened the cafeteria door, blew his whistle, and waved everybody inside.

"How is your mom?" I asked as we headed for the pep rally.

"Better. She's starting counseling. Her therapist wants us all to go."

"Are you going to?"

"I guess. It creeps me out, though, having to tell a complete stranger all our family secrets."

"At least your mom is facing up to the truth now."

"It's about time."

We entered the auditorium and found seats in the back row. Despite the early-season loss to Mirabeau, our team had clinched the conference championship the week before, so this last game was anticlimactic. Although you wouldn't know it from the way the cheerleader clones ran onto the stage yelling and clapping, then doing splits that looked downright painful.

"It's a blue!" they yelled, starting the cheer that

always opened the pep rallies. "It's a blue! It's a blue, blue, blue!"

Zane came in with Ginger and a couple of guys from the swim team. He waved to me and pulled Ginger onto a seat beside him.

Nick and I scrunched down and tried to talk above all the noise. Pep rallies never were among my favorite activities. Basically they're an ego trip for the jocks and the cheerleaders. Although a pep rally meant my PE class was canceled, always a plus.

"So," Nick said into my ear as the cheerleaders launched into another yell. "What are you doing for Thanksgiving?"

Normally, I loved Thanksgiving. Mama always went overboard on the fall decorations, filling the house with pumpkins, candles, maple leaves, and straw baskets overflowing with miniature squashes, grapes, and apples. She roasted a huge turkey and made corn bread dressing, sweet potato casserole, and cranberry relish from scratch. But this year she would be at a big sales convention in California. Shyla was going skiing with friends in Vermont, which left Daddy, Zane, and me to fend for ourselves. Daddy made great pancakes and excellent burgers, but let's face it, turkey and dressing demanded way more culinary skill than he possessed. I had no idea what he was planning for the big day.

"Maybe I could come over the day after," Nick said. "We could hang out. If you want."

It was the first time Nick had ever suggested hanging out at my house. I was thrilled to pieces, but I played it cool. "Sure. That would be great."

When school let out for the holiday the following Wednesday, Zane and I went home to find Daddy already in the kitchen, thumbing through a stack of Mama's cookbooks.

"Hey, Dad," Zane said. "What's up?"

"I was planning on fixing a traditional Thanksgiving dinner for us, but I'm afraid I may have started a week or so too late. Most of this stuff takes hours, if not days, to prepare. I don't see how your mother managed it."

"Maybe we can still get a reservation at the Eden Inn," I said. "Their ad in the paper last week said they were serving a buffet."

"That's an idea," Daddy said. "I surely will miss a good home-cooked feast, but this year we will have to make do."

Then, as if she'd been waiting for her cue, the doorbell rang and Beverly called, "Hey, Trasks! May I come in?"

"By all means," Daddy said. "Come on in."

"I can't stay long," Beverly said, sweeping into the kitchen. "I have a conference call scheduled at five, but I saw your car in the drive, Sum-nuh, and I just popped over to see what you all are doing for dinner tomorrow."

"We were just discussing that," Daddy said. "With Beth and Shyla away, we're thinking of eating at the inn."

"Eating at a *restaurant* on Thanksgiving? I have never heard of anything sadder than that. Thanksgiving is for families."

Zane said, "Well, ours is a little fractured at the moment."

"Oh, honey, don't I know it?" Beverly said. "That's why I came by. To invite you all to my house tomorrow."

"That's too much work," Daddy said. "I couldn't let you do that."

"It's no trouble at all!" she said. "They have places where you can order everything already prepared. You just bring it home, heat it up, and dig in."

I could see Daddy weakening, and there was nothing I could do to stop it.

Beverly could see it too, and she pressed her advantage.

"I thought we'd order the hard-to-fix things, like the turkey and stuffing, but we can bake our own pies. I'm very good at pecan pie. I use my grandmother's recipe." She laid her hand on Daddy's arm. "You'd be doing me a favor. Otherwise I'm going to be eating all by myself, and that's no fun."

"All right," Daddy said. "But only if you let me take care of the turkey."

"Done! The name of the caterer is Garden of

Eatin'. They're in the phone book." She glanced at her watch. "I must go, but I'll see you all tomorrow. Come over around ten, and we'll get started on the pies."

"Great," Zane muttered, fishing out his keys. "I'm heading over to Ginger's."

"Again?" Daddy said. "This is the third night in a row. You don't want to wear out your welcome, son."

"Now, Sum-nuh, don't fuss," Beverly said, taking Zane's side like she was his mother and this was an old argument. "You know very well that when you're sixteen and in love, there is no such thing as too much togetherness."

Zane ducked out the back door, banging it shut behind him. Beverly just smiled her boys-will-be-boys smile and said, "See you tomorrow."

By ten thirty on Thanksgiving morning Daddy and Zane and I were in Beverly's kitchen mixing dough, cracking eggs, and measuring out corn syrup for the pies. In the living room a fire crackled in the fireplace, and the TV was tuned to the Macy's parade in New York. Daddy and Beverly chattered like magpies as we worked. I measured out flour and shortening for the piecrust, keeping one eye on the TV parade. Zane had reverted to silent mode, doing everything Daddy asked with exaggerated politeness.

"So, Phoebe," Beverly said, handing Daddy a rolling pin. "How is freshman year treating you?"

"It's okay."

"What is the scintillating Mr. Clifton doing these days?"

"Same old thing. Still as boring as a box of rocks." I poured corn syrup into a measuring cup and put the lid back on the bottle. "Mrs. Grady is sticking to her lifelong rule of not smiling until Christmas."

Talking about Mrs. Grady reminded me of Nick, and I felt better, knowing I'd see him the next day.

Daddy finished rolling out the pie dough, rinsed his hands at the sink, and went to the closet in the entry hall to retrieve his jacket. Beverly sent Zane to the garage with a bag of kitchen trash. She poured the pie filling into the shells and added a cup of pecan halves to each one. "How are things with you and Nick?"

It was just one more question designed to worm her way deeper into my life, but I was so amazed that out of all the girls in the freshman class Nick had chosen me, I told Beverly the one thing I hadn't even told Shyla yet: that he had invited me to the Snow Ball, the freshman winter formal.

"That's wonderful!" Beverly carefully set the pies in the oven, programmed the timer, and closed the door. "Maybe we'll take another trip to Dallas after the holidays and shop for your dress."

"The dance isn't until the middle of February," I said. "My mother will be back by then."

Daddy came back into the kitchen. "I'm heading downtown to pick up the turkey. Anything else we need?"

"No, I think we're all set," Beverly said.

Zane and I helped Beverly set the table. Daddy came back with the food from Garden of Eatin', and we put everything onto platters and into bowls. Beverly took the pies out of the oven and left them on the counter to cool. Daddy said a quick blessing, which he never did at home. Then he carved the turkey and we dug in.

I had just taken my first bite of cranberry relish when a taxi pulled up to our house next door. Through Beverly's dining-room window we watched as the driver got out, popped the trunk, and set three suitcases onto the driveway. He opened the rear passenger door, and a woman stepped out, shading her eyes against the bright autumn sunshine.

Mama had come home.

"It's Beth!" Daddy said, rising from Beverly's table. Then he stood there like he couldn't figure out what to do.

Me and Zane muttered a hasty "Excuse me!" to Beverly and raced across the yard to where Mama was digging in her purse for money to pay the driver.

"Mama!" I launched myself into her arms, almost knocking her over.

"My goodness, Phoebe, you're strong as an ox." Mama laughed and untangled herself. She reached around me to hand the driver his money. He tipped his cap, got in the taxi, and backed down the drive.

She kissed me, then grabbed ahold of Zane. "Hi, baby."

Zane turned ten shades of red, but he grinned and kissed her cheek. "Hey, Mom. How's it going?"

"I've been better, to tell you the truth. Where's Daddy?"

"We were having Thanksgiving at Beverly's," I said just as Beverly and Daddy crossed the lawn.

Daddy hugged Mama and kissed her cheek. "What a wonderful surprise! You should have told me you were coming for a Thanksgiving visit! I'd have met you at the airport."

"I had to fly standby because of the holiday," Mama said. "I wasn't sure when I'd get here."

"That doesn't matter now," I said. "You're home. How long can you stay, Mama?"

"We'll talk about that later." Mama touched the scar above Daddy's brow. "Are you all right? How is your collarbone?"

"It's knitting nicely," Daddy said. "I'm fine."

"I would have come home when it happened," Mama said, "but you had to be stubborn about it."

"Well, I'm sure your family is delighted to have you home now," Beverly said, drawing her sweater around her shoulders. "And you're just in time for Thanksgiving dinner."

"I'm sorry," Mama said. "I didn't mean to interrupt."

"Nonsense." Beverly linked her arm through Mama's as if they were the best of friends. "Having you here makes the day ever so special for your family. Come with me, and we'll start over."

Daddy and Zane took Mama's suitcases into our house. Ten minutes later we were reassembled around Beverly's table. Beverly kept up a stream of conversation all through the turkey and dressing, and on through coffee and pecan pie served in front of the fire in the living room. There were a million things I wanted to tell Mama, but right then I was content just to look at her, at the way the sunlight brought out the blue of her eyes and the dark beauty of her hair. Dressed in gray wool slacks and a bright yellow sweater, Mama looked thinner than I remembered, but she seemed okay; she'd eaten two helpings of sweet potato casserole and an extra-large serving of the skillet beans from Garden of Eatin'.

When we finished dessert, Mama offered to help clean up the kitchen, but Beverly wouldn't hear of it. "I want you all to go home. You've got a lot of catching up to do!"

Daddy carried his and Mama's coffee cups to the kitchen and picked up his jacket. "Thank you, Beverly, for a wonderful dinner."

"It was nothing." She turned to Mama. "I hope you enjoy your visit."

As we started across the yard, Zane let Mama and Daddy go ahead of us and whispered to me, "What about Lucky?"

"Omigod!" I ran past them, pounded across the porch, and let myself in so I could keep Lucky from escaping and knocking Mama down. By the time I had calmed his puppy exuberance, Mama was coming up the steps, laughing at something Daddy had said.

When she saw me standing in the entry hall holding on to the collar of a fifty-pound mass of yellow fur, she stopped cold. "What," she asked, "is that?"

"Mama," I said, "meet Lucky."

I held on to my puppy's collar as we went into the living room. Lucky's feet scrabbled on the hardwood floor as he tried to get to Mama so she could pet him. Any new person was fair game as far as he was concerned. "Me and Zane found him on the highway. We saved his life."

"Oh, Phoebe," Mama said, sinking into her favorite chair by the window. "You know how I feel about dogs."

"He's not just any dog. He's special."

She sighed. "People always think their dog is special. But dogs stink, they shed, they pee on the rugs—"

"Lucky doesn't," I said.

Daddy said, "He's housebroken, Beth. Feebs has done a great job with him."

"Sumner, don't tell me I have to fight you, too." Mama sounded incredibly tired, but I didn't care. I wasn't about to give up my dog.

"I'm keeping him," I said. "You'll be gone again after this weekend. Surely you can put up with him for three days, and when you come back in February, he'll be older and even better trained. He's really smart."

Mama closed her eyes. "Yes, I'm sure he's a genius."

"Mama, you can't make her give him up," Zane said. "It's not fair."

Her eyes snapped open. "Life isn't fair. I am proof positive of that." Then she started to cry.

"Beth?" Daddy bent down and put his arms around her. "What's the matter?"

"Oh, this is so hard. I wish Shyla were here so I'd only have to say it once."

My breath caught. I just knew Mama had decided to divorce her whole family and stay with Bee Beautiful forever. Which would make Beverly Grace absolutely ecstatic. She could marry my father and move right in, without even having to change the monogram on the towels in Mama's bathroom.

But then Mama got ahold of herself and said, "I can't go back to Bee Beautiful."

"What's wrong?" Daddy asked.

"I have cancer," Mama said quietly. "I just found out a week ago. Since then I've been tying up loose ends at the company and looking into my treatment options."

I went numb remembering when Lauren's aunt Ella got cancer. We'd watched her go from a normal woman to a thin scarecrow with papery skin and no hair, and finally to a pale wisp of a person who one day slipped into a deep sleep and never came back. That couldn't happen to my mother. It just couldn't. Zane, Daddy, and I stared at one another, dazed, while Mama gave us the details of her illness and talked about the appointment she had already set up with a specialist in Dallas. Then Daddy called Shyla at her friend's house in Vermont and told her to come home.

When Nick called the next day, I told him my mother was home, but not the reason why. Zane and I had been the subject of too much talk at school ever since the beginning of the year; first there was all the discussion about the trial and then the attack on Daddy. I wasn't up to having people whispering about me again. Besides, as scary as cancer was, you heard all the time about people who had beaten it and ended up good as new. And Mama was scrappy; she wouldn't go down without a fight.

"I should probably spend time with my mom," I told Nick. "She's been gone a long time."

"Sure. No problem."

On the one hand I was glad he didn't give me a hard time for breaking our date, such as it was; on the other I was disappointed he didn't fight harder to see me. To fill the silence that followed, I said, "How is everything at your house?"

"Okay. We're supposed to have another family counseling session next week."

"Well, I guess I'll see you Monday, then."

"Yeah. Monday."

We hung up just as Shyla arrived. Mama and Zane were napping, Daddy was doing research on his computer. I went out to help her carry in all her stuff. She had taken three suitcases on her skiing trip to Vermont, and each one weighed a ton.

"How is she?" Shyla asked as we heaved the luggage onto the porch.

"She slept most of the morning. Daddy says the trip wore her out."

"No doubt. The airports are a zoo this weekend."

"Mama had to fly standby. I'm surprised you got here so fast."

"I cheated. My friend's father had access to a corporate jet and offered to fly me down."

"Wow."

"Yeah, it was pretty plush." Shyla opened the door and called, "Hey, Dad?"

He came out of his study, his glasses propped on his head. "Hi, baby. Let me give you a hand."

He carried her stuff upstairs and dumped it all in her room. Then Mama came into the hallway, still in her robe and slippers even though it was past noon.

"Mama?"

Shyla started to cry, and Mama held her firstborn, her favorite, just as she always had. "Don't cry, honey. Everything will be all right."

Later, over tea and tuna fish sandwiches, Mama said, "If I'm going to fight this thing, I'm going all out. The doctor in California recommended radiation right away, and then chemotherapy, and that's what I intend to do."

"Shouldn't you get a second opinion, Mama?" Shyla asked, pushing her food away. I didn't blame her. I couldn't eat either, thinking about what Mama was facing. "I mean, radiation *and* chemo seems so drastic."

"It is drastic," Mama agreed. "And I will get a second opinion next week, but right now it seems like my best hope."

"I'll drop out of school," Shyla said, "so I can be here to take care of you."

But Mama said, "Drop out when you're so close to graduating? Absolutely not!"

"But who will take care of you when the chemotherapy starts?" Shyla asked. "Phoebe and Zane will be in school all day, and Daddy can't shut down his court altogether."

"I'll hire someone," Mama said. "You have your whole future ahead of you. I don't want my illness to derail your plans. I couldn't live with that."

Which was basically what Daddy had said about Mama when he was in the hospital after the beating. I began then to look at my mother in a different light. I'd thought she was totally selfish to go off on her Bee Beautiful adventure and leave us to fend for ourselves, but now I saw that maybe she wasn't as self-absorbed as I had thought.

After the long weekend Shyla hitched a ride back to Austin with a friend who had come home to Eden for the holiday, leaving Daddy, Zane, and me to cope with what came next.

A week later Mama saw another doctor in Dallas,

who basically agreed with the one in California, and her treatments began. At first she was strong enough to move around the house and drive to the grocery store. Daddy told her she should save her strength, but Mama said it made her feel normal to shop for her family again. As the countdown to Christmas began, she and Daddy went to a couple of movies, and she drove herself to the library and the hair salon.

But the poison chemicals soon wore her down, and by the middle of the month she was too sick to do anything. On treatment days she came home looking pale and tired. A couple of days later the vomiting would start. And despite what she'd told Shyla, in the end Mama refused to hire a home health nurse. She couldn't stand for strangers to see her in such a state. So me and Zane and Daddy worked out a schedule so that one of us was with Mama most of the time.

For Daddy it meant rescheduling hearings at the courthouse and referring some of his cases to other judges. It meant getting up extra early to get Mama bathed and medicated for the day. For Zane and me it meant coming straight home after school to clean up the sickroom, coax Mama into eating, do homework, make supper, and then clean the kitchen afterward. The three of us worked as a team to do what had to be done, but at the end of the day when Mama was finally asleep, we withdrew into our separate shells to nurse our private fears and figure out how to deal in our own way. The house was quiet as a tomb. Even Lucky seemed subdued. Once in a while Zane would laugh out loud and then stop himself, as if he'd forgotten he wasn't supposed to be happy. It was an exhausting routine that left us all feeling short-tempered and definitely not in the Christmas spirit.

To be completely honest, as much as I loved my mother, I resented her too. Of course I understood it wasn't her fault she'd gotten sick, but because of it I had no life. Every morning I got up filled with a sense of dread, slogged through my classes, and came home to the smells of medicine and vomit. There was never time for anything normal, like going to the mall or catching a movie. And Mama lay on her bed in the dark, indifferent to our attention.

One afternoon I came home to find Daddy on his knees wiping a gooey purple mess off the floor. Mama was curled into a ball on the bed, her face turned to the wall.

"What happened, Daddy?"

"Your mother's having a little problem taking her medication today."

"What's wrong? Is she worse?"

Mama rolled over and sat up, her hands clenched. "Just stop it, both of you!"

"Stop what, Beth?" Daddy sponged up more goo and put down some paper towels over the damp spot on the carpet.

"You know!" Mama stared at us, wild-eyed. "Talking about me like I'm not even here."

"We're just worried about you, Mama."

"A lot of good that does!"

"What do you want me to do?" I cried. "It's not *my* fault you're sick!"

"Phoebe." Daddy handed me the sponge and pail. "Take these downstairs for me, will you?"

"That's right, Phoebe," Mama said. "Leave the room so you don't have to look at your sick, crazy mother."

Tears leaked out of my eyes. How could Mama be so mean to me when I was trying so hard to take care of her? "Nobody thinks you're crazy, Mama. But you have to take your medicine."

"I don't have to do anything."

Daddy nudged me toward the door. "Go on, honey. I'll be down in a while."

In the laundry room I washed out the pail and threw the sponge into the trash. Zane came in, saw my face, and said, "Mama's on the warpath again."

"She's mad at the whole world."

"Tell me about it. Yesterday she said her cancer was my fault because I'd stressed her out when I got in trouble last summer."

We went into the kitchen. I washed my hands and started taking stuff out of the fridge, even though none of us ate much anymore.

"Don't pay any attention to that," I said. "If stress caused cancer, this whole family would be sick."

Daddy came downstairs looking totally worn out. He ran his hand over his face and tried to smile at Zane and me. "Tough day."

I took a knife from the drawer and started slicing pears for his favorite winter salad. Tough, I thought, didn't even begin to describe it.

*

After I'd turned down three invitations from Ashley to go Christmas shopping, I finally told her why I couldn't go. And when Nick kept bugging me in science lab, saying that he knew something was wrong, I told him, too.

"Man," he said. "That's the pits. How much longer is she gonna be barfing and stuff?"

"Till her treatments are over at the end of February, I guess."

"But then she'll be normal, right?"

"If the treatments work."

"They'll work," he said. "They just have to."

Which made me even crazier about him. He often said the exact same thing I was thinking. Like we were two parts of the same person.

On the last day of school before Christmas vacation, afternoon classes were canceled so we could go caroling downtown. It was a freshman-class tradition at Eden High, going back forever, and Daddy insisted that I not miss it. Even though I didn't feel much like singing, it was a relief to be doing something normal.

We met in the choir room after lunch, and Mrs. Lavelle, the choir director, divided us into groups and handed out our song sheets. We climbed onto the bus, and Mrs. Cantrell came out to remind us we were representing our school and we should mind our manners downtown. She got off, and the bus pulled out.

I was in a group with Courtney and five other girls I didn't know. Nick was in a group with three girls and a couple of boys from his history class. When he tried to get Courtney to switch with him so he could be with me, Mrs. Lavelle caught him by the collar and led him back to his seat, all the time telling him how if people started switching groups, the entire system would break down, ending democracy as we knew it.

On the way downtown we practiced singing "The First Noel," "Santa Claus Is Comin' to Town," and "Winter Wonderland." The plan called for each group to sing at four businesses, and then we'd all meet to sing at the senior center across from the library, after which the seniors would serve refreshments. Then the bus would take us back to school, where Zane would be waiting to take me home.

The bus chugged down Commerce Avenue and stopped in the parking lot of the Budget Buy Discount Center. After Mrs. Lavelle had given us another round of instructions and warnings, we fanned out across town. With Courtney in the lead, my group headed for our first stop, a jewelry store in the middle of the block. The owner, Mr. Whitstone, stood in the doorway as we worked our way through our repertoire. When we finished, he clapped and said, "Thanks, kids. Have a merry Christmas!"

We sang at the barbershop and then crossed the street to serenade the staff and patrons of Bramasole, the nicest Italian restaurant in town. We'd had Mama's birthday dinner there the year before, and I'd been totally blown away by the gold light fixtures, plush carpet, and snowy tablecloths. Bramasole looked like something out of an Audrey Hepburn movie. The food wasn't bad either.

We crowded into the lobby, which was full of people waiting to have lunch. Every table was taken. Waiters ran around filling water glasses and bread baskets. The smells of rosemary and tomato sauce wafted through the air.

Courtney blew on her pitch pipe, and we launched into our first song. People quieted their conversations to listen. Waiters stopped in their tracks while we sang about snow and sleigh bells, and everyone clapped when we finished.

We were just about to start our second number when Courtney tapped my shoulder and said, "Hey, Phoebe, isn't that your dad over there?"

I followed her gaze to a small table in the corner,

partially hidden behind a huge silk flower arrangement, where my father sat, having lunch with Beverly. I couldn't tell whether he'd seen me and was trying to make himself invisible, or whether he was so wrapped up in Beverly he hadn't even noticed I was there, singing my heart out.

"You want to go over and say hi?" Courtney asked.

"No." My throat closed up. How *could* he, when my mother was deathly ill? In that moment I didn't know my father at all.

Somehow I got through the rest of the songs and the concert at the senior center. By the time Zane met me back at the school parking lot, I was so mad I could barely tell him what had happened.

"What are we going to do?" I asked. "Courtney saw them together! Now everyone at school will know."

"Courtney doesn't know Beverly," Zane reasoned. "If it comes up, just say Dad was having lunch with some lawyer from the courthouse."

"But he's going behind Mama's back."

"There's nothing we can do except try to keep Mama from finding out."

"Shyla will be home soon. Maybe she can straighten him out."

"I wouldn't count on it. Dad is in a world of his own these days."

Even though Daddy was dead wrong to be seeing Beverly, a part of me could understand his need to get away from everything that was weighing him down.

Zane switched on the car radio. "Other than the shock of seeing Rhett and Scarlett at Bramasole, how was the caroling?"

"It was okay. The seniors at the center really appreciated it. They said we sounded great."

"The seniors must not get out much."

"I think I've just been insulted."

Zane grinned. "Listen, I need to get Ginger something for Christmas. Let's go shopping tomorrow and forget all this other stuff for a while. It's driving me nuts."

We went by Gus's to pick up burgers for supper. When we got home, Mama was sleeping and Daddy was sitting in front of the TV reading the paper, acting all innocent. It was all I could do not to ask him how he'd enjoyed his lunch at Bramasole. After supper we scattered as we always did. In the long, weary weeks since Mama's arrival the silence and isolation had become such a part of our lives it was hard to remember that things had been different once. I brought Lucky into my room, and he curled up beside me while I made out my Christmas list. I didn't feel much like celebrating, but the next day Zane and I headed for the mall.

"I'm stumped," Zane said as we circled the mall, looking for a parking place. "I have no clue what to get Ginger for Christmas."

"How about perfume?" I asked. "Or a bracelet. Porter's is having a sale."

Secretly I was dreaming of getting a bracelet from Nick. Something I could keep forever. I'd been waiting for an opportunity to drop a hint, but so far he hadn't brought it up.

"Too personal." Zane jammed on the brakes as a huge SUV lumbered toward us, heading the wrong way. We idled there, waiting for the driver to realize his mistake and back up.

"Ginger's hard to figure out these days," Zane continued. "She wants to go out with me, but sometimes she says I'm smothering her and she needs her space. She'd totally freak if I gave her jewelry. She'd think it meant I wanted to marry her or something."

We spotted a pickup backing out of a space. Zane eased forward and put his blinker on.

"How about a new set of socket wrenches?" I asked. "Or a gallon of transmission fluid? Or a tire pressure thingy?"

"Very funny."

We got out and he locked the car.

"I don't know what to get Mama, either," Zane said.

I knew what he meant, but neither of us could say it out loud. The thought that this might be our mother's last Christmas lay unspoken between us. I couldn't forget that Mama had refused the present I'd bought last summer for her birthday. Maybe she'd reject a Christmas present too. But we agreed that it was important to carry on as normal a Christmas as possible, and normal in the Land of Trask meant a huge tree and a ton of presents done up in shiny bows.

We entered the mall and agreed to meet two hours later at the Christmas tree near the food court. I went to Porter's Department Store to take care of the easy people on my list. I bought gloves for Daddy and a tiny silver coffeepot for the charm bracelet Shyla had started back in high school. I figured once she became a famous lawyer, she'd like something to remind her of her barista days. For Zane I got a shirt from his favorite designer. Then I wandered around looking for the perfect present for Mama, hoping inspiration would strike. I checked out a couple of displays of silk scarves, pyramids of designer chocolates done up with gold bows, and rows of necklaces and pins nestled into velvet boxes.

Nothing seemed right until I got to the stationery department and saw a beautiful journal bound in red leather. All those blank pages just waiting to be filled made it seem like a hopeful present that someone in Mama's situation might appreciate. Although I usually wrapped everything myself, I paid extra to have the journal wrapped by the professionals in the customer service department.

I left Porter's and went to the bookstore across from Happy Feet. One of Nick's favorite pro football coaches had just published a new book called *Winning at Sports, Winning at Life.* I figured with everything Nick was going through at home, he could benefit from some solid advice from someone he admired. I bought the book and a leather bookmark with his initial on it. On my way to meet Zane I stopped at a kiosk selling gourmet dog treats and bought a giant peanut-butter-flavored bone for Lucky.

When I got back to the Christmas tree, Zane was already there holding two shopping bags and a cup of coffee. We didn't talk about our purchases as we headed for the car. It was a Trask family tradition to keep everything a secret until Christmas morning, when we'd gather after breakfast to exchange presents. Part of the fun was not knowing what anybody else was getting until the packages were opened.

When we got home, we squirreled away our purchases and raided the fridge.

"Phoebe?" Mama's voice, plaintive and thin as a wisp of smoke, drifted down the stairs.

Zane stuffed the last of his sandwich into his mouth and wiped his hands on his napkin. "I'll go if you want."

"No, that's okay." I drained my glass, set it on the counter, and went upstairs.

Mama was sitting at her dressing table, trying to tie a blue scarf over her hair. All the medicines she was taking had made her hair wispy looking, and she was self-conscious about it. She'd bought several scarves, and lately she'd taken to wearing them even when we were home by ourselves. Shyla said the fact that Mama cared about her appearance was a good sign. I was glad for anything hopeful to hold on to.

"Can you help me with this?" Mama asked.

I wound the scarf around her head and knotted it in the back.

"Thank you." She picked out a lipstick from her Bee Beautiful collection, spritzed herself with perfume, and checked her reflection in the mirror. "Did you and Zane have any luck at the mall?"

"I'm not telling. You'll have to wait until Christmas."

She smiled. "Daddy is bringing our tree home

tonight. And Shyla called. She'll be here the day after tomorrow in time for church."

"Great. I can't wait to see her." We Trasks were not especially religious, but we always went to the midnight service on Christmas Eve at Trinity Chapel, a little church about an hour's drive outside town. It was prettier than the huge, modern churches in Eden, which were made of brick and glass and looked more like discount tire stores or pizza restaurants than places to talk with the Almighty. At Trinity the walls were made of white marble with gold veins running through it, and there were twelve stained-glass windows depicting famous scenes from the Bible. During Christmas the altar was decorated with a life-size manger scene and tons of blazing candles that cast a soft, golden glow over the whole room. It made you feel like a better person just for being there.

Mama said, "Let's get the decorations ready."

We went downstairs. Zane helped me bring in the boxes of ornaments and garland from the garage. Mama lowered herself into her favorite chair.

Zane glanced at the watch Beverly had brought him from England. "Mom. Okay if I hang out at Will's for a while?"

"As long as you're back in time to help decorate the tree."

"Wouldn't miss it for all the tea in China." He kissed her cheek and left.

I opened the boxes and took out the ornaments, a mishmash of expensive crystal snowflakes, souvenirs from our trips, and stuff we'd made. There was a wooden apple with "I love NY" written on it, a plaster-of-paris nativity scene Zane had made in Cub Scouts, a set of miniature needlepoint stockings with our initials stitched on them.

Mama's face glowed as she relived the story of each ornament. We laughed at the paper plate with Shyla's first-grade picture glued in the middle, the edges soft and soiled from years of handling. "She was so proud of that," Mama said.

I unwrapped a miniature snow globe and the spun-glass star Zane and I had broken when I was six. The sight of it still made me sad because it was one of the few things left from my mother's childhood, and I was responsible for ruining it. When I knocked it off the tree playing chase with Zane, I was so upset I cried for an hour. Mama said it didn't matter, and we glued it back together, but you could still see a crack where the glue had dried.

I picked up a whelk Shyla and I had turned into an ornament one summer by covering it with glitter and ribbons. Mama had written the date inside. "Those were good times," she said. "I missed going to the beach this year."

"Me too. It didn't seem like summer without it." The memories and the soft Christmas music playing on the radio brought a lump to my throat.

Mama looked up. "What's the matter?"

"Everything was always the same, and suddenly it's all changed and I can't count on anything! How did our family get so messed up? Why did you have to leave and ruin everything?"

"I told you I was coming home in February."

"But I bet you wouldn't have if you hadn't gotten sick. Bee Beautiful would have offered you another great trip, and you'd have stayed away even longer. Maybe forever." Even to my own ears I sounded immature and whiny, but I couldn't help it.

"You think I left because I didn't care about you and Zane, or about your daddy. But that's not it. I just needed to feel like my life mattered too. I needed to know that I was still me. But I missed you every single day, even when I was too rushed to show it."

She opened her arms and we clung together like magnets, heart to heart. It felt good to be close to her again, even though deep down I was afraid to love her too much, terrified that she would die. I was glad that Mama couldn't read my mind just then; it would have hurt us both.

A police siren wailed. Lucky got scared and tumbled into the room, and before I could stop him, he laid his head on Mama's lap like she could save him.

"Lucky, no!" I grabbed his collar, but Mama just sighed and stroked his head.

"Never mind," she said, succumbing to his charms at last. "He can stay."

Daddy came home with our tree, and when Zane got back from the Hartes', we spent the rest of the evening decorating it. Later we made scrambled eggs and toast for supper and lit a fire in the fireplace even though it wasn't really that cold outside.

Then it was Christmas Eve, and Hurricane Shyla blew into town with bags of Christmas presents and a week's worth of dirty laundry. That night after supper when she went to the laundry room, I followed her. While she piled her things into the washer, I told her about seeing Daddy at lunch with Beverly at Bramasole.

"You always have some logical explanation for everything he does," I said. "But you don't see them together. The way they look at each other."

Shyla blew out a gust of breath that ruffled her bangs. "What do you expect me to do about it?"

"Talk to him. Tell him it's not fair."

"I'm sure he already knows that." She measured detergent and dumped it into the machine. "Sometimes people's feelings are so complicated they can't stop themselves, even when they know they should."

I thought about Nick's mom and the way she had

held on to her dream of a perfect life with Mr. Harper even after he'd proved over and over that he couldn't be what she wanted. I realized that when it came to the whole man/woman/love/sex thing, adults were just as clueless as teenagers.

Daddy stuck his head into the laundry room. "Girls? It's nearly time to leave for church."

"In a minute, Dad," Shyla said.

He closed the door, and Shyla put her arm around my shoulder. "I'll talk to him," she whispered. "Now, stop worrying. It's Christmas!"

The next morning I woke to the smell of pancakes and the sound of Christmas music playing in the den. When I got downstairs, Mama was already dressed in black pants, a red sweater, and a matching scarf. "Merry Christmas, Phoebe," she said.

"Merry Christmas, Mama."

Shyla helped Daddy make breakfast. Zane bounded down the stairs, and we started talking, eating, and laughing at once, just like old times. Afterward we went into the den to open our presents. Shyla appointed herself the official Santa. She stuck a red felt hat on her head and handed out each present with a dramatic flourish.

Zane swore he'd been very good, especially since finishing his community service hours, and Shyla handed him the box from me. He loved the shirt, as I knew he would. Then Shyla picked up a box and said,

"This one's for Dad. The truth now, Judge. Have you been a good boy this year?"

She looked straight into Daddy's eyes as she spoke. Zane and I exchanged glances. The fire crackled in the fireplace. In the background Elvis was crooning about a blue Christmas.

"The truth," Daddy said, "is that I haven't been as good as I should have or as good as I hope to be."

"Well, there's no time like the present to start mending your ways," Shyla said, handing him the package. "Merry Christmas, Your Honor."

An hour later we were sitting in a mountain of torn paper, empty boxes, and shiny ribbon. Lucky retreated with his new peanut-butter bone to his favorite spot in the kitchen; Zane took his loot, which included movie passes, a couple of sweaters, and half a dozen CDs, up to his room. I got pretty much the same assortment of stuff—books from Daddy, perfume and an awesome leather backpack from Shyla, a CD from Zane. Mama, who said she absolutely loved the red journal I'd given her, gave me a chunky turquoise and silver necklace suitable for a girl of my height and a complete line of Bee Beautiful products.

We were just clearing away the debris when the doorbell rang and Beverly, dressed in red velvet from head to toe, came in carrying a shopping bag. An expensive camera dangled from around her neck.

"*Buon Natale,* Trasks! I brought y'all a few

Christmas goodies to tide you over until suppertime."

"How nice!" Mama said.

"It was nothing. I was making fudge for the old folks' home anyway and figured I might as well make an extra batch." She set the bag down and said to Daddy, "Where's that good-looking boy of yours, Sumnuh? I'll snap a picture of you all while I have the camera loaded."

Behind her back I rolled my eyes at Shyla. Beverly always pretended she wasn't doing anything special for us, that we were just an afterthought in her superbusy life, but everything she did was calculated to bring her into contact with my father. The memory of their private little lunch at Bramasole knifed through me; still, when I remembered that Beverly was totally alone at Christmas, her husband and son both dead in a foreign country, I couldn't help feeling sorry for her. "You look really pretty," I told her. And I meant it.

Beverly's face lit up like I'd just handed her the moon and stars. "Why, thank you, sugar. I haven't worn this since . . . well, in a long while. I thought it was time."

"Yo, Zane!" Daddy yelled up the stairs. "Come down here a minute, son."

Zane came down and saw Beverly, and his eyes went hard. Daddy said, in his too-hearty voice, "Beverly wants to take a picture of our family."

"Zane, honey," Mama said. "Come over here and let me straighten your collar."

"It's fine." He turned to Dad. "Can we get this over with? I promised Ginger I'd be at her house by one o'clock."

"Then I'll be quick about it, Zane," Beverly said with an easy laugh. "Far be it from me to stand in the way of young love."

She motioned us into place. Daddy and Shyla stood behind Mama's chair. Zane and I stood on either side, and Lucky plopped himself down at Mama's feet. As we arranged ourselves for the camera, my mind filled with what-ifs. What if this was the last Christmas with Mama in the picture? What if Mama found out about Daddy and Beverly? What if the two of them ran off together? It was such an effort to smile that my face felt like it was about to break.

Beverly checked her light meter and fiddled with the camera. "Okay, everybody, smile!"

The flash went off. Beverly said, "*Va bene*. Good. One more."

She snapped another picture, and we scattered.

"Merry Christmas, Bev," Daddy said. "Thanks for the fudge."

As soon as she was gone, Zane left for Ginger's, and Shyla went to visit some of her old high school friends. Daddy offered to make lunch for Mama and me, but I was still stuffed full of pancakes. Plus, I couldn't wait a nanosecond longer to give Nick his present. I was about to explode, wondering what he had chosen for me.

I tucked his present inside my jacket and pedaled my bike to his house. A pickup was parked in the driveway. Through the window I could see a Christmas tree covered with foil icicles and blinking multicolored bulbs. On the front porch a little boy was playing with a set of miniature soldiers. I leaned my bike against the curb and started up the walk.

The boy stood up and squinted at me. "Who are you?"

"I'm Phoebe. I'll bet you're Jacob."

He nodded vigorously. "I'm four."

"I heard. Is Nick at home?"

Jacob dropped to his knees and picked up a soldier. "Yep." He looked up at me again. "How come you're so tall?"

"I don't know, Jacob. Just lucky, I guess."

"It's from eating vegetables, I bet."

"You're probably right," I said as the front door opened and Nick came out.

"Hey," he said. "What are you doing here?"

"It's Christmas." I handed him the book. "I brought you a present."

I was dying for him to open it. I knew he'd be totally blown away. But he just stared at me like I'd handed him a live snake.

"What's the matter?" I asked.

"It's just . . . I . . . I didn't get you anything, Phoebe."

"Oh." I felt like I'd been kicked in the stomach.

"I'm sorry. I mean, presents. I didn't think we were that serious, you know?"

I couldn't believe he said that. *What about the times we kissed?* I thought. *Didn't they mean anything? What about the time you came to the hospital when Daddy got hurt? What about the huge secret I kept for you?* All of it felt plenty serious to me, but I was too numb to say anything.

Jacob trotted over. "Aren't you going to open your present, Nick? It might be a computer game or a million dollars."

"Butt out, Jacob," Nick said.

I ran for my bike. "I gotta go. Merry Christmas."

"Phoebe, wait!" Nick called. But I pedaled away as fast as I could.

When I got home, I was too mortified to go inside. I parked my bike and got my old basketball out of the garage. I dribbled it on the concrete driveway, slapping the leather so hard my hands burned. I shot blindly at the basket, running and pivoting until I was breathless. I didn't know how long I'd been out there when I realized that someone was standing behind me, watching.

"Phoebe, what's the matter?" Beverly said.

"Nothing."

"You're crying. Is everything all right?"

I let the ball roll down the driveway and into the street. "Leave me alone!" I yelled. "Stop trying to act like my mother. You are *not* a part of my family!"

Even as the words were coming out of my mouth, I realized it wasn't only Beverly I was trying to punish, but I couldn't stop. "And stay away from my dad! He's married, in case you haven't noticed."

The back door opened and Daddy stuck his head out. "Feebs?"

I ran into the street and got my ball. Beverly turned around and walked back to her house. Daddy came outside. "Why are you yelling at Bev?"

"Why do you care?"

"What's the matter?"

"Everything!"

I set my shot, but the ball hit the rim and bounced back. Daddy caught it, pivoted, and let it go. The ball arced through the air and swished through the basket. Nothing but net.

Talk about awkward moments—picture my first day back in science lab with Nick after the Christmas disaster. I was already in a bad mood because Mama had yelled at me that morning for leaving the milk out of the fridge, and Zane was ticked because I had taken longer than usual getting ready and almost made us late for our first-period classes.

It was one of those days where one thing after another piles up, until it sets your teeth on edge, and after spending the entire lunch period listening to Ashley's blow-by-blow description of her entire Christmas bounty, followed by another of Mr. Clifton's painfully boring lectures on the founding of Rhode Island, I stomped into science class spoiling for a fight. I dumped my backpack on the floor, opened my workbook to the assignment on trilobites, and set out the microscope and specimens we'd need to begin our study of Paleozoic fossils.

Nick came in just as the tardy bell rang, and slid onto the stool beside mine. I bent over my book and pretended total fascination with drawing an arthropod.

"Hey, Phoebe?" Nick's breath was soft on my ear.

"What?" I adjusted the microscope and peered into it.

"I'm really sorry about, you know, Christmas and everything."

"Forget it. It was no big deal."

"Yeah, it was. I love the book. Coach Williams, man, he's always been my idol. I can't believe you knew that."

"It was a lucky guess."

Mrs. Grady strolled by our table and frowned. "Are you two planning to get any work done today?"

Nick opened his workbook, and Mrs. Grady went on to harass someone else. Nick said, "That book was the best thing I got for Christmas. It was a total surprise. I didn't realize you cared so much about me."

"Don't flatter yourself."

"Okay, you want to stay mad at me, fine. Stay mad."

"Thank you for giving me permission to have feelings!"

Mrs. Grady looked up. "Shhh!"

Nick said, "Are you finished hogging the microscope? I have to draw my examples too, you know."

"Be my guest!" I slid the microscope across the table, opened my textbook, and spent the rest of the period reading the same paragraph over and over.

*

It took a while, but by February, when Mama's treatments ended, Nick and I had reached a truce. We were talking again, but it sometimes felt strained. I wished I could go back to that first day of school, when everything was so free and easy between us. But now there was nothing about my life that was free and easy.

Even though the doctors had given my mother every reason to be optimistic about the future, she was still mad at the world and took out her anger on whoever happened to be standing in her path. As February dragged on, the warm Christmas feeling that had sprung up between Mama and me evaporated like the damp winter mist hanging over the river. She complained about everything—the way I folded the towels, the music Zane played in the den when he thought she was asleep, the temperature of the soup Daddy served for supper.

Daddy said it was a delayed reaction, that Mama was just now realizing how close she'd come to dying, and that her anger was a predictable response to everything she'd been through. Maybe so, but it still hurt to see my father, who was usually so happy and confident, withering under her constant verbal assaults. And it worried me to see how often he crossed the yard in the evening to sit on the porch with Beverly after Mama had gone to bed, their breath making little white clouds in the chilly winter air.

I couldn't blame him for wanting to get away from all the tension in our house, but I didn't see how he could turn his back on me and Zane when we needed his steadiness more than ever. As for Beverly, she hadn't come around much since Christmas. I figured she was working on another book; several times the parcel service guy had left oversize envelopes on her porch, and once I overheard her telling Daddy she was going to New York for meetings with her publisher.

At school all the talk was about the Snow Ball coming up the following weekend. Since Christmas, Nick had not said one word about it. I still wanted to go, even if my relationship with Nick wasn't the same, but I would have flossed my teeth with a razor blade before bringing it up and risking rejection again.

One afternoon Zane dropped me downtown on his way to Ginger's. I had a big project due in Mr. Clifton's world history class, and I needed colored folders and a new stapler. Lucky had chewed my old one to smithereens.

It was colder than usual for Eden in February, and I took a shortcut to the office supply store, which took me right past Sadler's Music Store. Sadler's wasn't as big as the chain stores at the mall, but they were known for their great selection and friendly service. They had three stores scattered across Texas, including the main one in Mirabeau, which had been there for almost sixty years. They specialized in hard-to-find stuff. Sadler's was where you went if you wanted an old recording by B. B. King, say, or the Everly Brothers.

I burrowed into my jacket, glancing into the window as I passed. And there was Nick. With a girl. She was wearing tight jeans, black boots, and a red leather jacket, and she and Nick were having a great time, laughing over a stack of CDs they were holding. For a minute I felt frozen in place, and that old kicked-in-the-stomach thing came back. I ducked my head so they wouldn't see me, and hurried down the street.

Half an hour later Zane showed up. I jumped into his car, slamming the door so hard the Ford rattled. More than usual.

"What's with you?" Zane glanced in the rearview mirror and eased away from the curb.

"Just tell me one thing," I said. "Why do boys *pretend* they like you and then go behind your back with somebody else? It's disgusting! You are *all* born missing the honesty gene."

"Not me," Zane said. "I've been totally honest with Ginger, and she still plays that come-here-go-away game with me. Half the time she acts like she's crazy about me, and the other half I might as well be living on Mars. Why can't *girls* be honest?"

"I was honest with Nick, and see what it got me."

"He's only fourteen," Zane said, like he was the ancient Dalai Lama dispensing wisdom. "Cut him some slack. It's tough being a guy these days."

"Oh, boo-hoo," I said, but then we both started laughing at the absurdity of it all.

The next day at lunch I bolted my pizza so I'd have time to go back up to my locker on the third floor. Mr. Clifton had finally worked his way up to the late 1700s and had assigned everyone a project. Mine was to write a report about the advances the American colonies made in the areas of science and religion. I learned, among other things, that in 1773, the first Public Hospital for Persons of Insane and Disordered Minds was established in Virginia.

I opened my locker just as a familiar voice behind me said, "There you are."

"What do you want?" I took out my report and slammed the door shut. A few other people had drifted upstairs after lunch, and the hall echoed with laughter and the clang of metal as lockers were opened and closed.

"I want to give you this," Nick said, handing me a thin, wrapped package. Without opening it, I could tell it was a CD. The sharp edges of the jewel box poked through the paper. It was obvious he'd wrapped it himself; the paper was ragged, and the tape was on crooked. There was no bow. "And I want to say I'm sorry."

I hated myself for going all teary eyed, but I couldn't help it. "Sorry for hurting my feelings at Christmas, or sorry for hanging out with that cute girl in the red leather jacket?"

"Emily?" Nick laughed, which made me mad all over again.

"I don't think it's funny."

"Would you change your mind if I told you she's my cousin?"

"Oh, please, you can do better than that."

He whipped out his cell phone and punched in a number. "Here you go. Ask her yourself."

I felt lower than a Paleozoic worm. "Never mind. I believe you."

He turned his phone off. "Open your present."

I handed him my history report and ripped the paper off.

"The Eagles! Their first recording! I can't believe you found this!"

Nick looked relieved. "It wasn't easy. I ordered it from Sadler's right after Christmas, and it took them a while to get it."

The warning bell rang and we headed for the stairs.

"Look," Nick said. "I need to know if you can forgive me."

"It's okay. Forget it."

"No, it isn't okay. I was just so surprised to get a present from you that I acted totally stupid about it. I know how you feel about me, at least I *think* I do. But I figured it was a mistake to like you too much. Look at Mom. She's like, completely in love with Pop, and he lets her down all the time."

On the second floor we stopped at the water cooler to let a bunch of people pass. Mrs. Cantrell came by with a couple of guys in suits; the varsity basketball cheerleaders hurried toward the gym carrying a huge banner they'd just finished making. To me it was just one big blur.

Nick said, "So anyway, I was wondering if you still want to go to the Snow Ball with me. I've already got the tickets and everything. I'm just not sure you want to be with me anymore."

I thought about what Zane had said about Ginger and about how girls have problems with honesty too. Even though I thought I probably belonged in the hospital for disordered minds, I decided to go for broke.

"I really want to be with you, Nick," I said as the bell rang. "More than anything."

His smile was worth every minute of the detention I had to serve that afternoon for being late to Mr. Clifton's class.

*

Mama had been in such a crabby mood, I almost didn't tell her about the Snow Ball, but looking back on it now, I'm glad I did.

"Oh, Phoebe, that's great," she said that afternoon when I went into her room.

A weak winter sun slanted through the partially opened shutters, casting a golden light on her face, reminding me of how beautiful she'd been before she got sick. She patted the bed, inviting me to sit, and I kicked off my shoes and curled up beside her, the way I used to when I was little. A thin book fell to the floor, and I picked it up.

"This is the book of poems I got for your birthday last year."

"I found it in the bottom drawer of my nightstand," Mama said, "and I recognized the wrapping paper. I hope you don't mind that I opened it."

"It's okay." I had totally forgotton about putting it there after the trip to Shreveport. That day in Louisiana now seemed a whole lifetime ago.

"I was happy to find it," she said. "Dickinson was one of my favorites when I was in college."

"How come you never told me you were a poet?"

"I don't know. I suppose I never really thought of myself that way. At first I wrote poetry mostly to make sense of my own feelings, and then when Shyla was little, I made up rhymes for her."

"But not for me."

"Sometimes I did, when you were really small. But as you got older, you seemed to prefer your daddy to me. I never thought it was that important to you."

"I thought it was because Shyla is your favorite."

"You are all my favorites. Never forget that, Phoebe."

She picked out a poem and read it aloud, her voice

lingering over the words until they sounded like music. She closed the book and kissed my cheek. "Now. Tell me all about Nick. What's he like?"

I told her almost everything, leaving out the scary parts about his dad. I told her about how smart Nick was, how all the teachers liked him, and about how he'd taken his little brother trick-or-treating at Halloween, and how he'd shown up at the hospital when Daddy got hurt.

"Do you have a dress already?" Mama asked when our talk circled back to the impending ball.

"Not really."

"Then, we have some serious shopping to do."

"Do you feel up to it?"

"Not right this minute, but we'll go early on Saturday when I have more energy and the crowds are smaller."

Which was exactly how it happened. Daddy and Zane both offered to drive us to the mall, but it seemed important to Mama that she drive herself. We were there when the stores opened at ten. A few people were buying stuff at the Presidents' Day sales, but Elegant Events, the specialty shop where Mama liked to buy her own clothes, was fairly quiet. She sat on a little gold-and-white chair while I modeled dress after dress. The one I liked best was short, strapless, and covered with sequins.

"That's too revealing," Mama said, and the saleslady nodded. Two against one.

"I like it." I twisted around to look at the back of it in the mirror. It *was* really short, but I loved the way it made my legs look even longer than they were. Deep down I knew Mama was right about the dress, but it felt so good to be sparring with her over clothes again that I kept it up a little longer. "If it were up to you, I'd still be wearing dresses with bows and sashes."

The saleslady shot Mama an aren't-teenage-daughters-a-pain look, then flipped through the rack and handed me yet another dress. "This just came in yesterday. It might work."

I tried it on. It was made of midnight blue satin, strapless, with a full skirt that made me feel like a princess. Mama's eyes filled when I came out of the dressing room, my yellow wool socks peeking from beneath the hem.

"Oh, Phoebe," she said. "It's perfect."

Which described both the dress and the day. After we bought shoes to go with my dress, we had lunch in the food court. Listening to Mama's happy chatter as we ate our salads, I felt like I was waking up at last from a long bad dream.

"I must remember to write this down in my new red journal," Mama was saying, "so I can look back when you're all grown up and remember how much fun we had today."

It was the first time Mama had mentioned her

journal since opening her present on Christmas morning, the first time she'd talked about the future.

As long as I didn't let myself think about the secrets I was keeping from her, secrets about Nick's family, about Daddy and Beverly, it felt like old times.

People say a picture is worth a thousand words, but even the photo the official Snow Ball photographer took of Nick and me can't do justice to that amazing night.

Nick and his mom came to the house to pick me up. I was still in my room getting ready when I saw their car pulling into our drive. I checked my lipstick one last time and went down to the living room just as Nick rang the bell. Mama let him in and embarrassed us both to death going on about how handsome Nick looked in his suit and what a darling couple we made. She posed us in front of the fireplace like department store mannequins while she fiddled with her camera, but something was wrong with the flash, and she finally gave up.

She and Daddy went with us out to the car, and they introduced themselves to Nick's mom, a thin blond woman with sad blue eyes. She smiled at me, spoke quietly to my parents, and introduced Jacob, who was strapped into his safety seat behind her.

Nick and I squeezed into the backseat; we escaped from Trask Land and arrived at school just as the deejay put the first song on.

Maybe it was all that fake snow and dazzling silvery light that made everything seem so magical. Whatever the reason, I was insanely happy because Nick and I were back on track after the whole Christmas fiasco. We danced every dance, hung out with Ashley and Courtney and their dates, and pigged out on canapés and chocolate éclairs.

Looking around at the other members of my class, I was surprised at how much we all had matured since the Howdy Dance last fall, when we'd stood around trying to look impossibly cool, secretly wishing we were somewhere else. Now everybody laughed and talked more easily, and the line to the girls' bathroom wasn't nearly as long.

Despite the hovering presence of about thirty chaperones, it was still the most romantic evening of my whole life, and when Nick managed to steal a kiss as we waited outside in the shadows for Daddy to pick us up, I was sure that nothing else would ever match the perfect joy of that moment.

"Did you have a good time?" Daddy asked as Nick held the car door open for me.

"Yes, sir," Nick said. I scooted over to make room for him. He shut the door and squeezed my hand in the dark.

Daddy pulled into a long line of cars snaking around the building and onto the street. "Looks like you had a good turnout."

"Mrs. Cantrell said almost two hundred students bought tickets," I said.

When we finally reached the street, Daddy said, "Nick. Your house is on Algonquin Street?"

"Yes, sir."

The conversation was so stilted I wanted to scream. For some reason Daddy seemed too tightly wound, and it worried me. To loosen things up, I said, "Is Zane back from his meet yet?"

"He came in around ten," Daddy said. "But don't ask him how it went."

"We got creamed," I said.

"Apparently so." Daddy put his signal on and turned left onto Thornton. "How about you, Nick? Are you into sports?"

"I played freshman football this year," Nick said.

"What position?"

"Running back. I scored two touchdowns."

"Good for you!" Daddy said in that overly enthusiastic voice adults use with kids. "What about next year? Going out for varsity?"

"Maybe. Mom says I need to hit the books if I expect a college scholarship. I know I'm not good enough to win a full ride as an athlete."

We pulled up in front of Nick's house, which was

dark except for the porch light illuminating the front door. Nick squeezed my hand again before opening the car door. "Thanks for the ride, Judge Trask."

"You're welcome."

I got into the front seat beside Dad and pushed the button to lower the car window. Nick leaned in. "G'night, Phoebe. It was fun. See you Monday."

He turned and jogged to the house. As we headed back through town, Daddy said, "So. Did the dance live up to your expectations?"

"It was awesome, Daddy. And Nick is so great."

"I'm glad you enjoyed yourself." He adjusted the heater vent. "Are you sleepy, Feebs?"

"Not really."

"Good. Because it's time you and I cleared the air." He swung through the drive-through at Gus's and got two coffees to go. Then we drove back to the park and pulled into the deserted lot. He turned the heater up another notch and handed me a coffee.

"I want to talk to you about Beverly," Daddy said, and the bottom dropped out of my stomach.

"What about her?"

"You've been angry with her since the beginning, and angry with me, too. I'm tired of feeling as if I should be defending my actions to a fourteen-year-old girl."

"You're an adult; you can do whatever you want."

"Nobody can do whatever they want. Everyone has limits." He sipped his coffee. The steam rose, fogging up the window. "Suppose you tell me what's been bugging you all this time."

"You really want to know?"

"I do."

"Fine. First off, it's the way you call her 'Bev' and she calls you 'Sum-nuh,' like you've been best friends forever. Second, Zane and I saw you in the car with her one day, and you lied about it."

"I lied about it? When was this?"

"Last summer. The day we found Lucky. We stopped to buy dog food and stuff, and we saw you and Beverly cruising down Main Street in her car, laughing like two wild hyenas. When I asked you where you'd been that day, why you were late, you said you'd had to run an errand." I sipped my coffee to clear the hard lump forming in my throat. "Some errand."

"I remember that," Daddy said. "And I remember the errand. The AC in this car went out, and I had to leave it at the dealership to be repaired. You and Zane were gone, and Beverly offered to pick me up."

I recalled the day I went snooping in Beverly's office and saw his initials on her calendar. To be fair, I guess it could have been just a reminder to pick him up from the car place. The morning after Zane's run-in with the law, Daddy drove Mom's van to work, but at the time I was so worried about my brother's troubles I barely noticed. "Maybe it *was* totally innocent. Why didn't you tell me?"

"There was nothing to tell."

"Okay, but what about your lunch with her at Bramasole at Christmas? Courtney and I *saw* you sitting with her. I was mortified. Plus it was really tacky of you to take her to Mama's favorite place. Especially when Mama was at home puking her guts out."

"Is *that* what it's all about? You think I'm seeing Bev behind your mother's back?"

"Well, I sure didn't see *Mama* sitting there with the two of you that day, and you never mentioned to any of us that you'd had lunch with Beverly. What was I supposed to think?"

"You were supposed to think," Daddy said slowly, "that your father would never do anything to hurt his family. You were supposed to think I have more honor than that."

"But—"

"Let me finish. That day at the restaurant I was waiting for Judge Capshaw to get here from Ellis County to discuss a case he's taking over from me. Beverly came in to meet her attorney, and he was running late. I asked her to join me for coffee while we waited for the two of them to arrive. If you'd stuck around for another few minutes, you'd have seen us going our separate ways."

The hurt in his voice made me feel about an inch tall. I scrubbed at a tear sliding down my cheek. "I'm sorry. It's just that you seem to have so much fun with her, and Mama was gone, and Beverly was at the house every day when you got hurt. Plus she showered us with presents for no reason, and it just felt like she was trying to take over and push Mama out of the picture."

"There's not a woman on earth strong enough to push Beth Trask out of the picture."

I set my cup in the cup holder on the console and rubbed my hands together. Across town a police siren wailed. The clock on the dashboard inched toward midnight.

Daddy said, "I'll admit Beverly came on strong, and it was unsettling at first, but when you remember that she's lost both her husband and her only child, it's easy to see why she'd be desperate for some kind of family."

"Well, I'm sorry for her. But still, she can't have *my* family."

"No." Daddy turned his cup around and around in his hands. "And maybe I have grown too fond of her. I was adrift when your mother left, and Beverly was someone to talk to. She was still grieving and needed somebody too. I consider her a friend, Feebs. A good friend. But that's all she is and all she'll ever be. Understand?"

"Yes." I let out my pent-up breath and shifted in my seat, feeling relieved and foolish all at the same time. "Have you told Shyla and Zane all this?"

"Not yet. But I intend to."

It had grown colder outside, and Daddy flipped the car heater to high. "Of course, I sensed months ago that something was bugging all of you, especially you and Zane, but I've been so busy with work, and with looking after your mother, that until tonight I didn't understand how serious the problem was."

"What happened?"

"I was outside talking to Beverly when Zane got in from the swim meet. He was in a bad mood, and when Beverly asked him how the meet had gone, he threw his duffel bag across the yard and yelled at her to butt out. When I insisted that he apologize, he refused. He asked me why I didn't just get a divorce and move in with Bev and get it over with. Then I realized how our friendship must have looked to all of you. And for that I am really sorry."

The thing about being a daddy's girl is that you put your father on a pedestal and spend your life looking up to him, expecting him to be perfect. Then something happens that sends him crashing down to earth, and you find out he's not superhuman after all, that he has flaws and weaknesses like everybody else, and you can't ever see him quite the same way again. Even so, you don't love him any less.

"Thank you, Daddy," I said. "Thank you for the truth."

"It's freezing in here," my father said. "Let's go home."

At the end of March, I turned fifteen. Shyla came home for my birthday, and we all went to dinner at Bramasole. It was a huge deal for me; now I was only six months away from getting my driver's permit. Last summer my future had seemed too far away even to think about, but now I could imagine myself starting my own life.

While we waited for our dinners, I opened the stack of presents beside my plate. It was the usual stuff—clothes, CDs, jewelry.

Looking at my family seated around the table, I thought about everything we'd weathered since my last birthday—Mama's absence and her illness, the trial, Daddy's beating, Zane's run-in with the law—and I felt a jolt of pride that somehow we had survived it all and glued our family back together again.

Not that my whole life was suddenly perfect. In a kind of weird cosmic trade-off I had my mother back, but I was losing Nick. His parents were splitting up, and his mom was moving Nick and Jacob back to

Houston, where their grandmother could watch Jacob while Mrs. Harper worked.

"Houston's not that far from Eden," Nick said. "We'll still see each other."

"Sure." I smiled like I believed him, but I'd seen too many of Shyla's boyfriends come and go to expect anything lasting with a fourteen-year-old boy. Still, Nick's news was a big shock, and I cried for three days knowing I would never forget him, the boy who had given me my first kiss.

Our dinners came, and after we had polished off salads, pasta, and rosemary chicken, the waiter took away our plates and came back with a huge Italian cream cake.

He placed it on the table in front of me and ignited a sparkler. *"Buon compleano, signorina!"*

Two couples at the table next to ours turned around and clapped. Mama, Daddy, Zane, and Shyla joined the waiter in singing the happy-birthday song, which was totally embarrassing and corny as all get-out, but also unbelievably sweet. I was growing up, but there was still enough kid in me to be thrilled at the sound of the familiar tune. Even though I tried not to show it.

Zane leaned across the table and handed me a flat package. "This is for you."

"But you already gave me the CDs."

"Yeah, but this is better."

I opened the package, which contained a single sheet of paper decorated with a red ribbon. "'The bearer of this certificate,'" I read, "'is entitled to unlimited driving lessons from world-famous instructor, Zane Trask.'"

"Wow, Zane! Thanks."

My adorable big brother ducked his head and grinned, happy to have trumped all the other gifts.

"The blind leading the blind," Shyla teased. "I didn't think they allowed minors to be driving instructors."

"I'll be almost eighteen by the time she's sixteen," Zane pointed out.

"You're both growing up too fast," Mama said, smiling at me across the table. "It's time you started thinking of your future, Phoebe. What do you intend to do with your life?"

"I don't want to think about that now. It's my birthday!"

"Well, you'd better think about it, missy. It's later than you think."

"Beth," Daddy said quietly. "Let her enjoy her birthday. We can talk about this at home."

"Don't you *dare* shush me, Sumner!" Mama flapped her hand at him, and her glass tipped over, spilling water and ice in my lap and all over the starched white tablecloth.

Shyla grabbed her napkin and blotted the water off my skirt. "Mama, please don't make a scene."

Mama started to cry. "All I did was ask a simple question, and all of a sudden I'm the bad guy!"

Several people in the restaurant turned around to stare at the birthday party that had suddenly turned into a disaster.

"Daddy, can we just go?" I jumped up and shoved my presents into the boxes they'd come in.

Daddy paid the check. Zane came around the table to help me. "It's okay," he whispered. "Don't let her get to you."

We left the restaurant and went out to the car, Zane and I carrying my presents, Daddy with his arm around Mama's waist, and Shyla bringing up the rear.

"I've been thinking," Daddy said as we exited the parking lot. "Spring break is coming up in a couple of weeks. I say we chuck everything and head for the beach."

"We're in," Zane said. "Right, Phoebe?"

"What about Lucky?"

"We'll take him, too," Daddy said, making his voice super cheerful.

Shyla unwrapped a stick of gum and popped it into her mouth. "Jazz-n-Java owes me a million hours of vacation time. I could fly out after my last class and meet you guys there."

Daddy said, "Beth, honey? Do you feel like making the trip?"

"Oh, do I get a vote?" Mama asked, her voice brittle with tears.

Zane edged forward and spoke so softly I had to strain my ears to hear him. "Hey, Mama? We're all sorry you've been sick. But do you think for one night you could think about somebody besides yourself and let your baby girl enjoy her birthday?"

Daddy pulled into the driveway and cut the engine. "The beach it is!" he said. "I'll make all the arrangements."

*

School let out on the second Wednesday in April, and the next morning we piled into Mama's van with our luggage, Lucky's crate, and enough junk food to feed an army. Daddy and Zane took turns behind the wheel. When Mama got tired, we stopped for the night. We arrived at our beach house around noon the next day. Daddy unlocked the door, and we hauled everything inside. The house looked just the way we'd left it. Mama's shell collection was lined up on the mantel over the fireplace. An old white vase sat on the breakfast table, waiting for fresh flowers from the flower stand on the Kerrison Parkway. A pair of Shyla's hot pink flip-flops were parked by the back door, which led across the dunes and down to the beach. While Lucky raced from one room to the other checking everything out, Mama opened the windows, and soon the house smelled of the ocean, a mixture of wet sand, seaweed, and salt.

Zane and I swept the floors and washed the beach towels and the sheets so our beds wouldn't smell musty. Zane leaned on his broom and inhaled deeply. "I love this place," he said dreamily. "When I'm on my own, I'm going to live here all the time."

"Better bring a boatload of money," Daddy said. "The insurance and upkeep will kill you."

Zane put the broom away and picked up his duffel bag. "Dibs on the sleeping porch."

"No fair!" I said. "You had it last year. Besides, I need the extra room for Lucky."

Zane fished a quarter out of his pocket. "I'll flip you for it."

"I shouldn't have to flip you for it. It's my turn."

Daddy went into judge mode. "It is her turn, Zane," he said. "And the room upstairs is really too small for two teenage girls. When Shyla gets here with all her things, we'll be stuffed to the gills."

In the past Zane would have argued about it, but now he just shrugged. "Okay, kid. You get the porch, I get the Boogie board first."

"Deal."

We changed into our swimsuits and took our beach towels out of the dryer.

Zane said, "Mama, come with us."

"I can't. We need groceries, and Shyla's plane gets here in a couple of hours. But I'm looking forward to our walk on the beach after dinner."

Mama and Daddy left, and Zane and I headed to the beach with Lucky. We jogged past knots of kids on spring break, old couples walking hand in hand, a few little kids building sand castles. When we got to one of our favorite spots, a wide curve of sand sheltered by dunes and oat grass, Zane plopped himself down and turned his face to the sun. "Man, this is great. *This* is what was missing from last summer."

"No kidding. It didn't seem like summer without coming here. I'm glad Daddy thought of it."

"After Mama's meltdown on your birthday he had to do something to keep us from coming totally unhinged."

"She seems happy to be here."

"Who knows what she's thinking?" He jumped up and grabbed the Boogie board. "I'm going in."

He ran into the waves, screaming as he hit the cold water. "Woo-hooo! It's freezing!"

I threw a ball for Lucky and scanned the water. It was calm near the shore, but farther out were a few rolling waves big enough for a good board ride. Zane paddled out and rode the wave in, yelling and pumping his fist in the air. He caught a few more waves, venturing farther out each time, until he was just a tiny speck on the water. Finally he came in, shivering a little, and handed me the board.

I slipped the rope over my wrist and paddled out. The water was chilly, but the afternoon sun warmed my bare back. I treaded water for a minute, just watching the pelicans diving for fish and the play of sunlight on the waves. I picked a wave and held on for the ride. Lucky raced up and down the beach barking at me. Just as the board touched bottom, a familiar figure emerged from across the dunes.

"Shyla!" I yelled.

Zane and Lucky reached her first. I heard Zane's excited voice and Shyla's bright laugh as she dropped to her knees to greet Lucky. I left the Boogie board on the sand and hugged her. She had slathered on a layer of Bee Beautiful tanning lotion, which smelled like summer at the beach, a mixture of honey and coconut.

"Hey, kiddo, how's it going?" Shyla brushed a blob of wet sand off my face.

"Okay." Everything seemed better now that my sister was home.

Shyla kicked off her flip-flops and tugged her white tank suit into place. "Come on, race you to the water."

We all took off running. Lucky raced ahead, then doubled back, yipping. Shyla dived into the ocean, swimming out to the deep water with easy, powerful strokes, Zane right beside her. I was never as good a swimmer as they were. I hung back, paddling around with Lucky, tossing his ball, enjoying the sun and the water, listening to the shouts of other people up and down the beach.

An hour or so later Daddy came down to the beach and waved us in. Zane propped the Boogie board on the back porch. I dried Lucky off and gave him a bowl of fresh water. While Mama rested, Shyla helped Daddy fix our traditional first-night-at-the-beach supper of corn on the cob, grilled shrimp, and sliced tomatoes, and I set the table with the mismatched china Mama had bought at a garage sale.

When everything was ready, I went upstairs to wake Mama.

She was already up and sitting at the window looking out at the ocean.

"Dinner's ready, Mama."

She nodded and held out her hand. I took it, and she pulled me down beside her. "Look. There's a young pelican learning to fish."

I watched the pelican glide above the surface and flop awkwardly into the sea.

Mama laughed softly. "He doesn't quite have the hang of it yet. Even though he thinks he knows what he's doing. But the adults won't leave him until he can make it on his own."

I'd been around Beth Trask for fifteen years, long enough to know it wasn't really the pelican she was talking about.

"I know I've got a lot to learn, Mama," I said. "But don't worry about me. I'll get it together one of these days and figure out my life."

Just then Daddy stuck his head into the room. "Beth? Feebs? Dinner's getting cold."

After supper Shyla said, "Mama, did you bring your camera?"

Every summer we took a bazillion beach pictures, which Mama saved in leather albums with the year embossed on the cover. If you wanted to know what Shyla looked like at age six with her front tooth missing, or what Zane looked like when he went through his punk-rocker stage a couple of years back, all you had to do was look in the albums.

Mama got the camera and tripod from the bag, set the timer, and took a couple of shots of us gathered around the dinner table. Then I took a few of Lucky and one of Daddy as he washed up the supper dishes.

Later we took our traditional first-night-at-the-beach walk and watched the sun set. Listening to the waves, watching the sky go pink and gold, gave me an easy, peaceful feeling inside. Shorebirds and sand crabs darted along the beach in front of us. Lucky ran ahead, snuffling at clumps of seaweed and the remains of a horseshoe crab lying half buried in the sand. He ran back to me with a stick in his mouth. I threw it and he took off again. Out on the horizon lights on shrimp boats winked on, and a few minutes later Daddy said, "It's getting dark. We'd better start back."

Zane whistled for Lucky, and we trooped back to the beach house. After we'd taken turns in the shower, we watched TV for a while, even though we could get only five channels and the picture was so wavy it was hard to see anything. Shyla grabbed a book from the pile of paperbacks we kept for rainy days. Mama fell asleep in her rocking chair. After the ten o'clock news Daddy woke her, and they went upstairs to bed.

Shyla and I left Zane watching some wiggly ninja movie on TV and headed for the sleeping porch, which was my favorite part of the beach house. It faced the ocean and ran the whole length of the house. Mama had furnished it with twin beds with white iron headboards and blue coverlets that matched the colors of the sea. Lying in bed at night, you could hear the breathing of the ocean as the tides ebbed and flowed, and in the morning you woke to ribbons of sunlight poking through the cracks in the old boards, the cries of the shorebirds, and the thrum of engines as the shrimp boats headed out for the day.

One summer my sister and I painted the ceiling pale blue and added a bunch of puffy white clouds.

Now the paint was faded, and some of the clouds were stained brown from a water leak that had happened one year during a hurricane, but I still looked forward to sleeping under the same roof my daddy had loved when he lived here with his aunt Reba.

Shyla fell onto her bed and laced her fingers behind her head. "Man, it feels great to be here."

"Yeah. I missed coming here last summer."

"I think Mama missed it too."

I climbed into my own bed just as Zane opened the door and stuck his head in.

"Are you two awake?"

"Barely," I said. "What's up?"

"I took Lucky out to do his thing. He's good to go till morning."

"Thanks, Zane."

"No problem." He patted Lucky's head. "Good night, dude."

"Zane?" Shyla said. "You want to run with me on the beach in the morning?"

"I'm going fishing with Dad. Thanks, though. G'night."

He shut the door, and a minute later I heard his footsteps on the stairs.

"Shyla?"

"Hmmm?"

"Tell me something."

We were lying half asleep on the sand under an umbrella, a cooler full of diet soda between us. Farther down the beach Zane and a couple of guys were playing keep-away with Lucky. Daddy was still at the house talking on his cell phone to his court clerk back in Eden. Mama had taken her camera and gone off on her own right after breakfast.

"Did you know that Mama used to write poems?" I asked.

"Sure. She used to make up rhymes for me when I was little." Shyla poured more tanning lotion onto her legs and rubbed it in. A couple of girls in skimpy bikinis ran by.

"How come you know all this stuff about her and I don't?"

"I don't know, Phoebe. It's not a big conspiracy or anything." She handed me the lotion and turned her back so I could smooth some on. "It doesn't matter anyway."

"Yes, it does." I finished oiling my sister up and handed her back the lotion. "I want to know everything about her. Mama never tells me anything about herself."

Shyla propped herself up on her elbows and pushed her sunglasses to the top of her head. "Some of it is pretty sad."

"Like what?"

"Well, once she told me about the year she was eight. She changed schools right before Valentine's Day, and she was the only kid in the class who went home without a valentine."

"That stinks. The teacher should have done something."

"No kidding. But that wasn't the worst. Remember my freshman year, when Mama and I drove all the way to Dallas to buy my dress for the Snow Ball?"

"I remember. Zane and I were jealous because we had to stay home."

"On the way back Mama told me how happy she was that I was going to the dance, because in all her high school years she'd never once been asked out. The night of her senior prom, while the other girls were posing for pictures in their formal dresses, Mama was home alone, watching TV in her sweatpants."

"Wow. I didn't know that." I remembered how happy Mama had been the day we shopped for my Snow Ball dress, and I realized that when my mother looked at me, she saw a chance to do over the parts of her life that had turned out all wrong.

Shyla flopped onto her stomach. "Mama can be difficult, but she loves us more than anything. Try to be patient with her."

"I *do* try, but she's always pushing me to make decisions I'm not ready to make. I'm only fifteen and I'm supposed to have my entire life planned out. What's the big hurry?"

"I think she's afraid of dying before you grow up, and she wants to know you're going to be okay."

"That's not a bad analysis, Shyla," Mama said from behind us. She dropped to her knees and peered inside our umbrella. "If law school doesn't work out, you can switch to psychology."

Shyla rolled over and sat up. "Mama, I'm sorry. I was just—"

"It's all right," Mama said, motioning with her camera. "Can I come in?"

"Sure." I scooted over to make room for her on my towel.

Shyla said, "You want a soda or something?"

"Not right now." Mama drew her sweater around her shoulders. "I'm a bit chilly."

She took my face in her hands. "Your sister is right, Phoebe. I do worry that if I go too soon, if I'm not here to guide you, you'll make the wrong choices and spend your life regretting it. That's the thing I fear, more than I fear dying."

"But you're getting better," I said. "You aren't going anywhere for a long time."

"No guarantees," Mama said.

"Nobody gets a guarantee," Shyla said. "I've got everything all planned out, but I could fail the law school entrance exam or get run over by a bus. But I promise you, Mama, if anything happened to you, I'd help Dad look after Phoebe. Zane, too. Don't worry about us."

"Yeah, Mama," I said. "Don't worry about us. We're Trasks."

Mama nodded like she didn't trust herself to speak. Then she looked at her watch and said, "My goodness, look at the time. Your daddy will be wondering where we are."

We shook the sand off our beach towels, packed up our stuff, and went back to the house.

Daddy and Zane were outside on the deck, grilling burgers on the old hibachi we'd had since I was a baby.

Lucky was lying as close to the grill as he dared, hoping a burger would fall his way.

"Hey, girls," Daddy called as we crossed the dunes, Mama in the lead. "How's the beach today?"

"Great," Shyla said. "I like coming here in April. It's less crowded."

Mama set her camera on the table. "I got some good shots of the dunes earlier. But the sunrise was obscured by clouds."

"I'm all sticky," Shyla said. "I'm going to take a quick shower."

"Don't be long," Daddy said. "The burgers are almost ready."

While he tended the burgers, Zane and I went to the kitchen for buns, mustard, and a bowl of watermelon chunks he'd left chilling in the fridge. We set everything on the picnic table, and I went back to get plates and glasses. Just as I was setting the table, Shyla let out a blood-chilling scream. "Oh, my God! Come quick!"

Daddy dropped his spatula and we all ran inside. "What's the matter?"

"Look!"

Shyla pointed to the fuzzy image on the TV screen, and there was my mother, big as Dallas, right there on the Beauty Channel. Mama-in-person clutched her hands to her chest and stared at the screen like she'd seen a ghost. But I guess it *would* be totally weird seeing yourself on television.

". . . and all it takes is a thin layer of our new Bee Gone concealer, and those fine lines and age spots disappear like magic." TV Mama finished applying makeup to the model and smiled her Bee Beautiful smile into the camera.

"What—," Zane began, but Daddy shushed him.

"And remember," TV Mama said, "if you call right now, you'll get the Bee Beautiful bonus pack, which includes our Bee Gone concealer, Moisture Glow night cream, and two lipsticks from our new collection, all in this beautiful travel tote."

Then the Beauty Channel hostess stepped into the picture. "This is an amazing offer, Beth," she said. "Folks, the calls are pouring in, so if you want to take advantage of this incredible collection of Bee Beautiful products, pick up the phone right now and dial the number at the bottom of your screen. There's less than a minute left to place your order."

The camera zoomed in for a close-up shot of the hostess. "Now, don't you dare go away," she said. "In the next hour we'll be bringing you the Howard Carmichael hair care collection. He's showcasing some great new products that I know you won't want to miss."

Then a car commercial came on. Shyla switched off

the TV and said, "Wow, Mama, you looked great on TV!"

"I taped that piece almost five months ago," Mama said, "and this is the first time I've seen it. I thought they'd decided not to use it."

"They'd be crazy not to use it," Zane said. "You're the best saleslady Bee Beautiful ever had."

Mama pulled Zane close and kissed him. "Thanks, honey."

Daddy said, "Who wants lunch?"

We headed outside. I was starving, but the burgers were ruined, burned beyond recognition. Even Lucky realized they were inedible.

"Hand me your keys, Dad," Zane said. "I'll go pick up a pizza."

"I've got a better idea," Daddy said. "Let's drive into town for lunch."

A couple of hours later we were sitting at a table overlooking the harbor, drinking sweet tea and eating shrimp and grits. After we'd finished off the meal with peanut butter pie, we walked down the cobblestone streets to the waterfront, past the pink- and blue-painted houses and the Gullah ladies selling their sweetgrass baskets. I took pictures of my family in front of the famous water fountain, and after a walk around the Battery we started home.

Zane conked out in the backseat. Mama and Shyla were talking to Daddy. I switched the camera on and reviewed the pictures we'd taken that week. There were shots of Shyla and Zane flying a kite at sunset, pictures of Daddy walking on the beach with his shoes in his hand and his pant legs rolled up to the knees, and the pictures of the five of us Mama had taken with the tripod and timer.

Shyla said something that made Mama laugh and for a moment I wondered if Mama loved us as much as Shyla thought. After all, Mama was a master of deception, a wizard who could take lipstick and concealer and turn anyone into a whole new person. But the more I thought about it, the more I realized all of us were keeping secrets of one kind or another. When it comes to the people in your life, what you see may not necessarily be what you get.

Our last day at the beach passed too quickly. We swam with Lucky, played beach volleyball with a group of church kids from Mississippi, and pigged out at a low-country boil. Mama and I walked to Mingo Point, talking and taking pictures, and the last of my doubts melted away.

"Stand over there," Mama directed when we'd crossed a low bridge spanning the river. "I want a picture of you with your hair like that."

"Are you kidding?" I smoothed my hair off my face. "It's a mess."

"It's windblown," Mama said. "It looks very

fetching." Then she laughed at herself. "Do people use that word anymore?"

"I don't know."

She focused and pushed the button, and the camera beeped. "Very nice," Mama said. "You're becoming a real beauty."

"Me?"

We started walking again.

"Yes, you." Mama looped her arm through mine, and I felt her trembling. "I owe you an apology."

"What for?"

"For lots of things. For starting the Bee Beautiful job without explaining to you why I had to do it. For spoiling your birthday. And for making those unkind remarks about the necklace Beverly gave you."

"I put it away, Mama. I haven't worn it all year."

"Well, that's a shame, because it's lovely. I didn't mean to disparage Beverly's gift. I was jealous that someone else was paying attention to you, even though I was the one who chose to leave." She let out a long breath. "Anyway, I'm sorry."

"It's okay. It doesn't matter now."

Beneath the bridge a silvery fish broke the surface of the water and landed with a soft splash.

"Come on," Mama said, wrapping one arm around my waist. "Let's start back."

Walking on the beach later that last night, I found a

couple of whelks, empty and perfectly formed, and added them to the collection on the mantel. Zane and I helped Mama close up the house while Daddy drove Shyla to the airport for a late flight back to Austin. The next morning we packed the car and went home.

A couple of weeks after we returned from the beach, the police arrested two guys for the attack on Daddy. It turned out they weren't from Eden at all; they belonged to a group from Houston that called itself the Global List of Radical Youth, GLORY for short. According to the police chief, their purpose was to protect the American flag by beating up on anyone who dared desecrate it. These mental giants couldn't figure out that the ideals behind the flag were way more important than a piece of cloth.

Anyway, I was hugely relieved that nobody connected with Nick's family was involved; Nick already had too much stuff to deal with. His dad had left Eden. The Harpers' house was up for sale, which meant Nick had to keep his room clean all the time in case buyers came to check it out. While they were waiting to move back to Houston, his mom was working the night shift at a convenience store on the Dallas highway, and Nick had to hurry straight home after school every day to babysit Jacob.

"At least you won't have to watch Jacob after you move," I said one day as we ate lunch in the quad. "Your grandmother is going to take care of him, right?"

"Yeah, but I need to find a job for the summer, to help Mom with my school expenses."

I thought about my own plans for the summer—sleeping late, hanging at the mall with Ashley and Courtney, maybe even taking a trip to Atlanta to see Lauren, and I felt so bad that Nick would have to spend his vacation working instead of just kicking back and enjoying being fifteen.

Finally freshman year wound down. Madame Rochard gave exactly one A in French One. Personally, I was relieved to escape with a B. The week before classes ended Mr. Clifton finished lecturing about his glorious tapestry and wound up showing a series of jerky classroom films, which several people slept through. Courtney and I sat in the back row of his class and wrote notes back and forth, planning our summer vacation. Mrs. Grady handed back our final projects in science class. Nick and I got an A and celebrated by consuming ice-cold sodas and a giant package of M&M's.

In PE everyone had to repeat the physical-fitness test, to measure how far we'd come since last fall. Ashley, Courtney, and I managed to climb the rope but were told we still needed to work on increasing our endurance over the summer.

Ashley leaned over and whispered, "The only thing I'm working on this summer is my tan."

"Ditto." Courtney flipped her hair and checked it for split ends. "I wonder if that avocado shampoo I saw on TV really works."

"I'll bring you some Bee Beautiful shampoo," I said.

"Girls!" the teacher said. "Either your attention, or *de*tention. I don't care which."

We stopped talking and finished inking in the charts that showed how many push-ups, sit-ups, and chin-ups we could complete in five minutes.

That Friday, Zane went with the rest of the junior class to their end-of-the-year blowout at Six Flags, leaving me to ride the bus home after school. Beverly waved as I crossed the street, and I went over to say hello.

Behind her on the porch were piles of boxes. Following my gaze, Beverly said, "I'm moving."

Even though everything had been straightened out, I was relieved at her news. But at the same time I felt guilty that maybe I had contributed to running her off.

"Where are you going?" I let my backpack slide to the ground.

"Back to Italy," Beverly said softly, shading her eyes with one hand. "After Marshall died, I thought it best to find someplace new and start over, but now I realize it's useless to try to outrun your memories. It just doesn't work."

"Maybe you'll be happier in Italy."

"My husband always said if you can't be happy in Italy, you can't be happy anywhere. But I don't know. I've decided to keep this house for now. Maybe someday I'll come back and try again."

"What will you do over there?"

"I'm not sure. Maybe I'll paint, or write another book. Maybe I'll become a winemaker and spend my days stomping grapes. Anyway, I was wondering if you'd have some time tomorrow to help me pack my books. The movers will be here next Tuesday."

"Okay, sure." I picked up my backpack.

"And Phoebe? I'm sorry if I caused you any problems. I didn't mean to."

"I know. I'm sorry I was rude to you. I was all mixed up about a lot of things, and I took it out on you."

"Don't worry about it." She patted my arm. "You're a sweet girl. I'll miss you."

"I'll see you tomorrow."

"Great. Hey, wait! I have something for you. Be right back."

I waited while she ran inside and came back with a manila envelope. "Here you go. Open it later."

I shouldered my book bag and crossed the yard to our house. Mama was out back, kneeling in the dirt with her watering can and a package of flower seeds. Lucky was lying next to her, his tongue hanging out. She looked up and smiled when I came though the gate.

It felt good to see Mama looking so much more normal. Her hair had come back white and curly, which made her look totally different, but somehow it suited her. She looked happy even with a dirt smudge on her cheek and black potting soil caked under her formerly perfect Bee Beautiful nails.

There were other changes too. Since our trip to the beach Mama had been writing in her red journal every day. Now she was planting seeds that wouldn't push through the soil for weeks, another hopeful sign.

She handed me a trowel and said, "Dig me some holes. Lucky and I are planting zinnias."

Lately Mama had been hanging out with Lucky like he had been her idea all along. And sometimes he acted like he was hers instead of mine. But I wasn't complaining. I scratched his ears and set my backpack down. The envelope Beverly had given me slipped onto the ground. Mama picked it up. "What's this?"

"Beverly gave it to me."

"May I open it?"

"I don't care."

Mama slit the envelope, and the photographs Beverly had taken at our house back on Christmas Day spilled out. There was Lucky, sprawled on the floor with his legs straight out behind him and a goofy grin on his face, blissfully unaware of how close he had come to being roadkill. Behind him stood the five of us. I could see the scar on Daddy's forehead, Mama's thin, shadowed face, and Shyla, Zane, and I looking hopeful despite our bruised hearts.

Like the old stones in the wall in Connecticut, we had done a lot of shifting that year, but we were still a family; still holding each other up. Who cared if we weren't picture perfect? If you look close enough, you can see cracks in everything. And that's okay. Because when you really think about it, it's the cracks and gaps and chinks in things that let the light shine in.